JUST WILLIAM – AS SEEN ON TV

Just – William a facsimile of the first (1922) edition
The William Companion by Mary Cadogan
The Woman Behind William: a life of Richmal Crompton
by Mary Cadogan
Just William's World – a pictorial map
by Gillian Clements and Kenneth Waller
School is a Waste of Time!
by William Brown (and Richmal Crompton)

"DO YOU KNOW WHO I AM?" THE STRANGER SAID
MAJESTICALLY.

"NO,' SAID WILLIAM SIMPLY. "AN' I BET YOU DON'T KNOW
WHO I AM, EITHER." *(see page 48)*

Richmal Crompton

*Just William –
As Seen on TV*

ILLUSTRATED BY THOMAS HENRY

M
MACMILLAN CHILDREN'S BOOKS

This collection, first published 1994, by
MACMILLAN CHILDREN'S BOOKS
A division of Macmillan Publishers Limited
London and Basingstoke
Associated companies throughout the world

ISBN 0–333–62802–0

Phototypeset by CentraCet Limited, Cambridge
Printed in Great Britain by
Cox & Wyman Ltd, Reading, Berkshire

Contents

Chapter 1

William and the Russian Prince

The Brown household was moved to its depths when Robert received an invitation to the cricket week at Marleigh Manor. For Marleigh Manor – unlike most of the large houses in the neighbourhood, which were now inhabited by wholly successful if only partly educated tradesmen – was a stronghold of aristocracy, and its cricket week was a social event.

Robert paled on reading his invitation.

"But, good heavens!" he gasped. "I shan't know what to do. I mean – well, you know, I simply shan't know what to *do*."

"Why not, darling?" said Mrs Brown. (Mrs Brown was the sort of mother who could not imagine her children at a disadvantage in any circumstances whatsoever.) "You play cricket so nicely."

"I know I do," said Robert modestly, "but that's not the point. A *week*. Butlers and footmen and that sort of thing. And people with titles. I – well, I shan't know what to *do*."

"Nonsense, dear," said Mrs Brown. "All you have to do is to be just your own natural self."

But Robert had less faith in his own natural self than Mrs Brown had.

"It's all very well to say that," he rejoined gloomily, "but – I shan't know what to *do*. I mean, half the people there will have valets."

William's face lit up.

"I say," he said eagerly, "s'pose I go with Robert and pretend to be his valet."

"Nonsense, dear!" said Mrs Brown.

"I'll go as his butler, then," said William. "Honest, they'd think a lot more of him bringin' his butler with him. I bet all the high-up people take their butlers with them when they go to stay at places."

"Nonsense, dear!" said Mrs Brown again.

"If you come within a mile of the place while I'm staying there," said Robert savagely, "I'll wring your neck."

"All right," said William distantly, "I was only tryin' to help you. That's all I was tryin' to do. I'd make a jolly fine butler. So don't blame me if no one takes any notice of you there."

"No, I won't," said Robert, and added bitterly: "And I don't want the sort of notice people take of me when you're anywhere about. I've had enough of that to last a lifetime, thank you very much."

"Now, children, don't quarrel," said Mrs Brown mildly; "there's a lot to arrange if Robert's going. Perhaps you ought to have a new white waistcoat for your dress-suit, ought you, dear?"

William walked away, leaving them to an animated discussion of Robert's wardrobe.

For the next few days he preserved an aloof attitude, an

attitude that said more plainly than words that he had given Robert his chance and Robert had not taken it, therefore Robert could now stew in his own juice. But he was not really as aloof as he appeared. Secretly he was deeply interested in this opening of the strongholds of aristocracy to Robert and anxious to do something to further Robert's prestige within them.

"Couldn't I go as his page if he won't take a butler?" he said to Mrs Brown.

"Don't be so silly, William," said Mrs Brown patiently. "People don't have pages nowadays."

"Well, it might start a fashion and make him famous," retorted William.

"Nonsense, dear!" said Mrs Brown.

"Which is highest," said William, after a pause, "Sir or Duke?"

"Duke. Why?"

"Well, I thought I'd write to Robert while he was there and put Sir Robert Brown or Duke Robert Brown on the envelope; whichever's the highest. Or what about Earl?"

"William, you mustn't do anything of the *sort*," said Mrs Brown, aghast. "Robert would be *furious*."

"Well, I can't think why. If it was me goin' there I'd arrange with someone to do that while I was there. I wouldn't mind paying someone to do that – to send me a letter every day with Duke or Earl on. If Robert wasn't so mean he'd give me a sixpence a letter for doing it. And then I'd put Buckingham Palace, London, on it too, and cross it out as if he'd been staying with the King an' was havin' his letters sent on from there. Seems to me Robert hasn't got any sense. If it was me I'd have them all thinkin' I was the most high-up person there by the end of a day. I'd be spendin' all the time now writin' envelopes like that for people to post to me 'stead of fussin' cause there's a patch on one pair of pyjamas, and the stripes go the wrong way on the other, like what Robert's doing."

"I'm making him a new pair of pyjamas," said Mrs Brown apologetically. "It's only in one sleeve that the stripes go the wrong way. I was using up an odd bit of stuff and really I can't see even now that it matters so terribly. However—" The "however" evidently meant that tirades of eloquence from the nervous Robert had convinced her that it did.

"After all," she ended, "it's very good flannel, and personally I don't think anyone would notice that the stripes go the wrong way on just that one sleeve."

"Why don't you embroider coats of arms and things on his clothes?" said William thoughtfully. "That would make him seem more high-up. I bet all high-up people have coats of arms an' things embroidered all over their clothes."

"Nonsense, dear!" said Mrs Brown once more.

"Seems to me," said William bitterly, "no one wants to help Robert but me. You won't let me go as his page or his butler or send him high-up letters, an' you won't even embroider coats of arms an' things on his clothes. Well, I've done my best and I hope you won't blame me if no one takes any notice of him there."

Mrs Brown promised that she wouldn't, and William relapsed into an offended silence.

He watched Robert morosely when the fateful day arrived, and Robert, looking pale and nervous and carrying his suitcase, set off to walk the few miles that separated his home from Marleigh Manor.

"I don't expect that anyone'll even *speak* to him," he muttered despondently. "'Tisn't even as if he *looked* high-up. An' if he'd let me help he'd've had 'em all callin' him Your Royal Highness an' suchlike as soon as he got there."

"NO ONE WANTS TO HELP ROBERT BUT ME," SAID WILLIAM
BITTERLY. "YOU WON'T LET ME GO AS HIS BUTLER, AND YOU
WON'T EVEN EMBROIDER COATS OF ARMS ON HIS CLOTHES."

When a day had passed without news of Robert, William's
curiosity became more than he could endure, and he set off
by a circuitous route to Marleigh Manor. Cricket was in full
swing on the cricket field, and William crept along in the
ditch till he was just behind the bench where he could see
Robert sitting watching the game. On two wicker chairs
some distance from the bench sat Lady Markham, the
chatelaine of Marleigh Manor, and by her side a hook-nosed
crony armed with a *lorgnette*.

"My dear," Lady Markham was saying, "I simply don't
know who half the people are who are staying in the house.
One doesn't nowadays. My husband meets a man in a train

– in a *train*, mind you – who's interested in old coins – my husband has a *wonderful* collection, you know – and promptly asks him over for the week. He's all *right*, of course. A charming man. And he's brought his secretary with him. He's writing a book on old coins and the secretary's taking notes and making sketches of my husband's collection. But really, you know, when I was young, people simply didn't ask casual acquaintances to their houses without knowing anything about their families. And half the young men Ronnie's asked for the cricket I've never seen before, and never even *heard* of their people."

William passed on noiselessly in his ditch. Sir Gerald Markham sat a short distance away next to a grey-bearded, benevolent-looking old man who was evidently the coin enthusiast.

"Of course," Sir Gerald was saying, "no coins compare in interest with the Roman coins. I have, I believe, one of the earliest in existence. They weren't struck at all, you know, under the Empire . . ."

William moved on to where Robert sat rather forlornly at the end of the bench. Next to him was a youthful beauty of the peroxide blonde type and a tall youth with dark curling hair. The two of them were evidently engrossed in each other. And Robert was as evidently attracted by the blonde beauty, who seemed, for her part, unaware of his existence. William took in the whole situation at a glance. He had not been Robert's brother for eleven years for nothing. His heart burnt for Robert, thus neglected and ignored. It was his own fault, of course. If Robert had only taken him as butler or page, if Robert had that morning received a letter addressed to Earl Robert Brown and apparently forwarded from Buckingham Palace, if he had been able even now carelessly to draw up his trouser leg and reveal the top of his sock embroidered with a coat of arms, the attitude of the blonde beauty, William, knew would be very different. It was Robert's own fault, and yet William felt it his duty to extricate him, if possible, from the morass of nonentity and neglect into which he seemed to have landed himself. He crept away, his brow knitted, his freckled face wearing an expression of grim purposefulness. He must go very carefully, of course. Robert must know nothing of his efforts. If Robert knew of them he would certainly do his best to thwart them, so obstinate and pig-headed was he even when it was a question of his own good.

William went to his back garden, sat on an upturned flower-pot, his chin in his hands, the faithful Jumble lying by his side, and unavailingly racked his brains for a plan. At last he gave up the attempt in despair and, fetching the penny shocker that he had begun in bed last night (the keyhole stuffed with cotton wool, the mat pressed tightly up against the door, to hide all traces of the crime), lay down at full length on the lawn and went on with it.

And the penny shocker, as if to repay him for the risks he had run on its behalf, gave him his plan.

The blonde beauty – whose name, by the way, was Clarinda Bellew – walked slowly down the field towards the wood that bordered it. It happened that all the eligible and good-looking youths of the party were playing cricket, and she was feeling bored. She was tired of hearing her host dilating on his unique collection of coins and her hostess lamenting the deterioration in the manners and deportment of the young since the days of her own youth.

She was passing the point where the wood joined the field when she heard a loud cough and turned with a start to meet the fixed stare of a small boy, crouching behind a bush.

"WHAT ARE YOU DOING HERE?" SHE SAID HAUGHTILY.
"I'M ON GUARD," SAID WILLIAM.

"What are you doing here?" she said haughtily.

"I'm on guard," he said.

"On guard?" she repeated, impressed despite herself by the unflinching earnestness of the small boy's gaze. He was obviously no youthful trespasser caught red-handed.

"Yes . . . There's a Russian prince playin' cricket with those people an' I've been told by Scotland Yard to guard him."

"You!" The blonde beauty struggled with her amazement. "But why you?"

"Well, you see," said William, "they thought that no one would think it funny to see a boy hanging round watching a cricket match, but a policeman or plain-clothes man would make people sort of suspicious. I'm a good deal older than what I look, of course. I've been kept small by Scotland Yard so as to be able to take on jobs like this. Anyway, I'm supposed to be watchin' this Russian prince to see no harm comes to him."

Clarinda's blue eyes had grown wider and wider during this recital. Like William she fed largely on sensational fiction. Moreover, she was a regular attendant at the "pictures". Such a situation as William described was nothing to the situations that she swallowed daily without question on the films or in novels. And William's frowning purposeful gaze was almost hypnotic in its convincingness.

"Which one is it?" said Clarinda wonderingly.

William looked over to where the game was going on.

"It's that one . . . the one that's batting now."

They both gazed at the unconscious Robert for a few moments in silence.

"B-b-but," stammered Clarinda, amazed, bewildered, deeply intrigued, "I thought that he was someone who lived over in the next village."

William laughed – a short grim laugh.

"Oh, yes, that's what he's *supposed* to be," he said. "He was rescued from the revolution when he was a boy and brought over here secret and given to this family to pretend he was their son so as to keep him in hiding. You see" – William's voice sank to a sinister whisper – "you see, the Bolshevists are after him. He got away with all his jewels for one thing, and they're after his jewels." He warmed to his subject as a fresh and thrilling idea occurred to him. "You see that very dark man over there?" and he pointed to the youth who had engrossed the maiden's whole attention to the exclusion of poor Robert the day before.

"Yes," she said excitedly, "it's Theo Horner."

"Well, he's a Bolshevist. He's after the jewels. That's why I'm told to guard this Russian prince against him."

"But what could you do?" she said, looking down at his small stocky figure.

He assumed a mysterious expression.

"Oh, I've got ways," he said. "I've got secret signals. I could have all Scotland Yard here in no time if I gave some of my secret signals."

His eyes met hers unflinchingly, and the last of her doubts disappeared. After all, she'd always believed that things like this were happening all round one all the time if only one knew where to look for them. Life couldn't really be as dull as it seemed on the surface. All the thrills couldn't really be confined to the cinema. Well, here was one in real life – a thrill as big as any she'd ever seen on the pictures.

The situation resolved itself quite simply in her mind into the usual triangle – herself the heroine, Robert the hero, Theo the villain. She gazed reflectively at Robert, who – an agile figure in white flannels – was running across the pitch after hitting the ball clear of the fielders.

"One might have known," she said dreamily. "He looks an aristocrat. Every inch an aristocrat."

"You won't tell anyone, will you?" said William anxiously. "I mean – well, they'd probably get him at once if they knew anyone knew."

"Of course," said Clarinda, her very soul athrill. "Of course I quite understand that.'

"You see," hissed William, "your life'll be in danger too if anyone finds out you know."

Clarinda closed her eyes in silent bliss. From the age of ten, when she had attended her first film, she had been longing for someone to say something like that to her.

"I'm not afraid," she said, making her eyes as big as

possible and seeing an imaginary "close up" of her face wearing its proud brave smile. "I've never known what it is to be afraid."

"And most of all," William said, "you mustn't let him know you know."

"The prince?"

"Yes, the prince. If he knew you knew he'd go straight away an' none of us would ever see him again."

"No, of course I won't," she said, doing another imaginary "close up" even better than the first – a "close up" in which the dreamy gaze of dawning love was mingled with the proud brave smile. She already saw herself as a Russian princess, loaded with jewels of fabulous value. She would be deeply involved in international plots. By a daring *coup*, which would make her one of the most famous figures in history, she would overthrow the Soviet and restore her husband to the throne.

When she awoke from this dazzling vision she found herself alone. The small boy had disappeared. She walked back to the others in a slightly dazed condition. It *had* happened, of course? It wasn't all a dream? That small boy hadn't been pulling her leg? No . . . she recalled his earnest face, his determined frown. No, he couldn't have been pulling her leg. The story sounded impossible, but not half as impossible as things that had actually happened in history and were printed in black and white in history books. Not to speak of the films . . .

Robert was surprised to be greeted by her with a dazzling smile when he returned from the cricket pitch. Theo was equally surprised to be greeted with cold indifference.

"Do come for a little stroll with me," she said to Robert, fixing her blue eyes upon him. "One gets so stiff just hanging about."

"I'd love to," said Robert.

She drew a deep breath.

How courtly his manners were, how princely his bearing! She might have guessed . . .

Robert was slightly distrait, which, of course, added greatly to the air of mystery with which Clarinda had already invested him. What was he thinking about? She wondered. About the princely surroundings of his childhood, which, of course, he could not have forgotten? About the dangers among which he now moved? About the great *coup* that might restore to him his fallen fortunes? As a matter of fact, Robert was thinking about the entertainment that the cricket eleven was to give to the rest of the house party at the weekend. One item was to be a skit on Hamlet, and Robert had been chosen to represent Hamlet. He had been given a script of his part to learn and had been sworn to the utmost secrecy on the subject. It was a point of honour with the Marleigh Manor Cricket Team that no single piece of information about their programme should leak out before the actual performance. They boasted that in all the years that they had been holding the cricket week with its grand finale of the dramatic entertainment, the programme had never leaked out yet.

"They'll all try to worm it out of you," they had warned Robert, "but keep your mouth shut about it whatever you do."

Robert had kept his mouth shut about it, but he was nevertheless feeling guilty and ill at ease, for he had left the script of his part in the library that morning for over an hour and was terrified that someone might have come in and read it. He had rushed back to retrieve it as soon as he had discovered its loss and had found it just where he had left it, but – suppose someone had been in the interval and seen it and already the news was common property? At the thought that it might be he who had broken the tradition of years, completely disgracing himself by his carelessness, the perspiration broke out on his brow. Clarinda thrilled as she watched the obvious signs of his uneasiness and mental distress. So should a man look who carries his life in his hands, a man surrounded on all sides by his own enemies and the enemies of his race. It was all eminently satisfactory. Suddenly she decided to let him know that he had at least one friend in the network of foes that surrounded him. She laid her hand on his arm.

"Don't look so worried . . . Prince," she said.

The blood flamed into this face. She knew. She knew that he was to be Hamlet. She'd been into the library and read his script. The others would never forgive him. He was disgraced for ever.

"You know?" he gasped.

"Yes, I know," she said sweetly.

"You . . . I say, you haven't told anyone, have you?"

"No. Not a soul," she assured him with the ravishing smile.

Poor boy, how young he looked to live this life of constant deadly danger.

"You – you won't tell a soul, will you?" he pleaded. "I mean – well, I shall be simply *ruined* if you do."

"I know," she said. "I know all about it. You can rely on me. I shan't tell a soul. And I'll never mention it again even to you."

But she couldn't resist adding: "Have you got the jewels with you here?"

It so happened that Hamlet's outfit included a large

amount of "jewellery" that had been purchased for the occasion at the Woolworth's branch of the neighbouring country town.

"Yes," answered Robert innocently. "I've got them upstairs in my bedroom."

Clarinda closed her eyes and drew a deep breath of ecstasy. It was all too marvellously, marvellously film-like. She decided to tackle Theo, too, before the day was out. Just hint to him that she knew what he was up to . . . not to say anything definite, of course.

She found him after tea reading a novel on a wicker chair on the terrace. He put down his novel and sprang to his feet eagerly.

"I say," he said, "come for a walk with me, will you?"

She took up his novel, opened the fly-leaf and read the name, "Theodore Horner."

"I wonder what you'd say," she said slowly, "if I told you that I *knew* your name wasn't really Theodore Horner."

The blood flamed hotly into the young man's face, and he shifted his eyes from hers in unmistakable guilt. Since the day he went to a public school he had been striving to hide from his contemporaries the fact that the name Theo by which he was known was short, not for Theodore, but for Theodosius. He had inadvertently revealed this fact at his prep school, and his life there had been in consequence a protracted persecution. Learning wisdom from that, he had always afterwards pretended that his name was Theodore. But now this girl had evidently discovered the truth, and there were plenty of people at the house party who could, he knew, make the name the theme of unending witticisms. And he was a dignified young man, who disliked being ragged.

Clarinda gazed at him sternly.

"Well?" she said.

"Don't tell anyone, will you?" he pleaded.

"No," she said, "I've already promised not to do that. But – remember I know, that's all."

With that she turned on her heel and left him.

But the deep glance she had sent from her blue eyes before she left him increased his enslavement. She knew that his name was Theodosius, but she'd promised not to tell, and she wasn't the sort of girl to rag one, so it was all right . . . She was *jolly* pretty, and she'd really seemed quite to take to him. He'd ask her to go for a walk with him before dinner. He went in search of her and found her playing a single with Robert. She played with Robert till dinner-time and after dinner danced with Robert till bedtime. The next day she and Robert were inseparable, and the bewildered Theo was snubbed unmercifully whenever he approached her. He couldn't understand it. She'd been simply ripping to him till she'd found that his name was Theodosius and then she'd changed suddenly and completely. It was jolly unfair. Theodosius was a potty name, but, after all, it wasn't his fault he'd been christened it. Girls, he decided not for the first time, were frightfully queer.

William, of course, hovered near to keep an eye on the very satisfactory results of his handiwork. Robert would have been surprised and horrified had he known how often his dallyings with the divine Clarinda were closely watched by William from the refuge of the ditch, or the bushes outside the window of the Manor. William was becoming bolder and bolder in his expeditions. He kept well out of Robert's way, and no one else seemed to take any notice of him. Once he ran full tilt into the benevolent-looking coin enthusiast as he was rounding a corner of the shrubbery. He assumed his mock fatuously imbecile expression and said:

"Please, sir, may I just look round the garden a bit?" and the benevolent-looking coin enthusiast had patted his head and replied benevolently:

"Certainly, my boy, look round as much as you like."

William treasured the permission as something to fall back upon in case of need.

He was delighted to see Robert basking in the favour of the blonde beauty, but there was no doubt that trouble was brewing from the quarter of the dispossessed suitor. For Theodosius had quickly passed from a state of bewilderment to one of aggrievement and from one of aggrievement to one of active resentment. This Brown fellow had simply pinched Clarinda from under his nose and flaunted his victory with open exultation. Well, he – Theodosius – wasn't the sort of chap to put up meekly with that sort of thing, and he'd jolly well *show* that Brown fellow so before he'd done with him. Every night in his dreams he pummelled poor Robert with monotonous regularity, and every day he followed Robert about with a ferocious scowl that made even Robert, uplifted as he was by Clarinda's sweetness, feel slightly nervous.

Clarinda herself, who now lived completely in the Russian-prince dream, accepted Theo's attitude quite simply as that of the Red Russian thirsting for the White Russian's blood – not to speak of his family jewels.

"You know," she said to Robert, "I do think you ought to be careful. He looked at you like murder then. Where do you keep them?"

"What?"

"The jewels."

"Oh, those." (Extraordinary how girls' minds could hop about from one subject to another.) "Oh, I've got them upstairs."

"Well, you *will* be careful, won't you?"

"Yes, rather! of course I will," promised Robert vaguely.

Then, because Robert's aristocratic birth belonged to the past and his possible‾ conflict with his enemy to the future, and because, after all, the present was really more interesting than either, they fell to discussing the films they had seen recently and, by a natural process of reasoning, passed on to Clarinda's resemblance to the film stars whom Robert most admired. It was while they were engaged in this absorbing conversation that Theo passed and directed upon Robert a look so venomous that Clarinda felt something must be done at once to avert the tragedy that seemed to be threatening the exiled prince.

It was quite by change that she ran into William, crouching in his hiding-place in the shrubbery waiting for an opportunity to approach the window and watch the progress of the situation he had so successfully created.

"Oh, there you are!" she said. "I was just wondering how to get hold of you. I say, you know, thngs are getting serious. I think you ought to *do* something . . ."

"What can I do?" said William, taken off his guard for a minute.

"I thought you were in constant communication with Scotland Yard," said Clarinda.

"Yes, I am," agreed William hastily, "yes . . . yes, of course I am."

"I suppose you can communicate with them by wireless any time?" went on Clarinda, whose knowledge of wireless was rudimentary in the extreme, and who, in fact, imagined it to be some mystic means of communication independent of any instrument.

"Oh, yes," said William, "oh yes . . . I can do that all right."

"Well, do you know," she continued earnestly, "I really

think you ought to be on the spot. I mean, you never saw anything like the way that villain's glaring at him. I do wish he hadn't got the jewels with him."

"Yes," agreed William, "I told him that was a mistake, but he was scared of leaving them anywhere else."

"Yes, of course, I quite understand that. But – well, I think that you ought to be on the spot, so as to be able to communicate with Scotland Yard at once in case of danger. You see, I'm frightened of tonight."

"Why?" said William. "Is it the play tonight?"

"No, that's to-morrow," said Claudia, "and I'm not worrying about that. I don't even know whether the prince is in the play at all." (It thrilled her to say "the prince" casually like that.) "But tonight is the dance we're giving to the village cricket team in the barn, and we're having a little dance ourselves there first before they arrive, and – well, I'm nervous. I think the Bolshie may take the opportunity either to steal the jewels or to do something to the prince. I suppose there's a deadly vendetta between them!"

"Oh, yes," said William vaguely, "oh, yes, there's that all right."

"Well, I think you ought to be on the spot. Look here, how about telling Lady Markham everything and asking her advice?"

William's blood ran cold at this prospect.

'Oh, no," he said earnestly, "that would jolly well spoil everything. Rob – I mean the prince would go away at once if she knew. I mean, I've sworn to keep it secret, and if anyone finds I've told even you I'd prob'ly get put in prison for life, An"' – he sought for a more horrible prospect as Clarinda seemed unmoved by this – "an' prob'ly the prince'd get put to death by torcher."

She shuddered.

"Perhaps you're right," she said. "Perhaps we ought to go on keeping it a secret. Well, will you be outside the library window tonight at half-past eight?"

"Yes," promised William, "I'll be there."

Promptly on his arrival at the library window that evening it was opened cautiously by Clarinda.

"Are you there?" she whispered.

"Yes," hissed William.

"Well, look here. We're all going down to the barn for that dance in a minute, but – you'd better come in now and hide behind the curtain here. He's been glaring most horribly all through dinner, and we may need you before we go down. You slip in here. I'll come back as soon as I know when we're going."

William entered the room and took up his post behind the thick velvet curtains. After a short interval the door opened and two men entered. He peeped cautiously from his hiding-place. It was the benevolent-looking coin enthusiast and the young man who was his secretary. The secretary carried a small case.

"Got the key?" said the elder man, and his voice was no longer mellow and benevolent. It was curt and urgent.

"Yeah," snapped his secretary and took a key from his pocket. Together they opened a safe in the wall, took out several trays of coins, and, picking out one here and one there, put them into the small case. The collector then slipped the case into his pocket.

"I'll keep it on me," he snapped. "Safer."

"Let's clear off now," said the other as he closed the case and pocketed the key.

"Don't be a darned fool," replied Benevolence. "I'm going

down to the barn with the others and in half an hour you can come in and tell me I've had an important telephone message from town. Then we'll get off at once . . ."

"Right."

They went out. William had been too much occupied by fear of discovery to listen to this conversation. The men had been in, taken some coins from a safe, and gone out without finding him. That was all the incident meant to William – alas for his frequent dreams to catching criminals red-handed!

After a few minutes Clarinda reappeared.

"Nothing's happened yet," she whispered. "We're going down to the barn now. I think you ought to come too. I believe there's a loft."

"Yes, there's a loft all right," said William, who knew all about the barns for miles around, "an' there's a ladder up to it outside."

"Well, I think you ought to be there," said Clarinda. "I have a sort of feeling that things are going to come to a head to-night. I must go now . . . You *will* be there, won't you?"

"Yes," said William, "I'll be there all right."

After all, he reasoned, he could easily escape from the loft by the outside ladder if things came to too much of a head . . .

He slipped through the kitchen garden to the barn and climbed the ladder to the loft. There he withdrew the trap-door and gazed down at the long decorated room. The house party was assembling. Robert and Clarinda, deeply engaged in confidential conversation, stood just beneath the trap-door. Theo approached them. Ignoring Robert, he fixed his eyes on Clarinda.

"May I have the second dance with you?" he said.

Clarinda's blue eyes flicked him up and down contemptuously.

"I'm afraid I'm engaged for all the dances this evening."

"To this chap?" sneered Theo, baring his teeth in the approved fashion of the villain through the ages.

"That's no concern of yours," said Clarinda icily, turning away from him.

Theo, too, turned away, deliberately jostling Robert as he did so.

"Look where you're going, can't you?" said Robert angrily.

For answer, Theo jostled him again. Robert hit out. Theo hit back. Clarinda screamed. All was tumult and confusion. The guests separated the two fighting men and held them apart. Clarinda stepped into the middle with flashing eyes.

"It's time the truth were known," she said dramatically. She turned imperiously to Robert.

"Let me speak, Prince . . ."

Robert blinked at her in bewilderment. She pointed an accusing finger at Theo. "That man's name is not Theodore Horner."

"Shut up," muttered Theo fiercely.

"Do you deny," went on Claudia, "that you are going under an assumed name?"

"No, I don't," shouted Theo, "but I don't see what business it is of yours."

"Well, I'll show you what business it is of mine," said Clarinda. She pointed to Robert and, turning to the assembled company, announced: "This man is a Russian prince."

Robert gaped at her.

"No, I'm not," he said.

"Oh, I *know* I promised to keep it secret," she said, "but

"DO YOU DENY THAT YOU ARE GOING UNDER AN ASSUMED
NAME?" DEMANDED CLARINDA.

"NO, I DON'T," SHOUTED THEO, "BUT WHAT BUSINESS IS IT OF
YOURS?"

don't you see – they must know – now that he's attempted your life."

"He hasn't attempted my life," said the literal Robert. "He's only given me a sock in the jaw."

"He's a Russian prince," went on Clarinda, again pointing to Robert. "He escaped from the revolution as a child with his family jewels, and this man" – she pointed now to Theo – "is a Bolshevist who has pursued him ruthlessly from his cradle."

"That's a lie," said Theo.

"You've just admitted that you're going under an assumed name."

"Yes, but that's not the same as being a Bolshevist and pursuing people from their cradles."

Sir Gerald suddenly stepped forward to take charge of the situation.

"What's your real name?" he said to Theo.

Theo hung his head in shame.

"Theodosius,"

"Horner?"

"Yes."

Sir Gerald turned to Robert.

"And are you a Russian prince?" he said.

"No," replied Robert.

"Why did you tell her you were?"

"I didn't."

"Who did, then?"

It was at this moment that William, already leaning dangerously far out of his trap-door, engrossed by the dramatic scene beneath him, was startled by a rat running over his legs, overbalanced, and fell down upon the assembled company. He picked himself up. Robert's face became a frozen mask of horror.

"He did," said Clarinda, pointing to William. "He's a detective in constant communication with Scotland Yard and he's been told to guard the prince."

Sir Gerald took firm hold of William's ear.

"Who gave you permission to come here?" he said grimly.

William remembered the permission that he had treasured against this occasion.

"*He* said I could," he answered triumphantly, glancing round the circle of guests for the white-bearded man. "*He* said I could come whenever I liked. I can't see him now, but he was in the library a minute ago putting coins out of the safe into his pocket."

Almost immediately the benevolent-looking old gentleman, abandoning his air of old age and benevolence, leapt from behind the circle of guests to the open door. Sir Gerald made a grab at him as he passed, but he escaped, leaving the patriarchal beard in Sir Gerald's hands. Theo pursued him, and flung himself upon him. He received a blow in the eye that sent him running back to the others for safety. Robert joined the pursuit, outstripped the others, seized the thief, received a blow that sent him staggering, sprang to his feet, received another that almost blinded him, continued the pursuit, caught the thief once more, was thrown off and kicked, continued the pursuit, and managed at last to hold him till the others came up.

It was later in the evening. The dance was in full swing. Robert, black-eyed and bandaged, was sitting out with Clarinda.

"I can't tell you how sorry I am about the whole thing," he was saying. "It's all that little devil's fault. I'd no idea—"

"Well," said Clarinda thoughtfully, "just at first I was sorry to find out you weren't a prince, but, when one comes to think of it, it would have been a very difficult life for us both. I mean, surrounded by enemies on every side and that sort of thing. No, I'm glad really that things have turned out as they have . . ."

She was silent, gazing dreamily in front of her. It was quite film-like after all. A different type of film from the other, but quite definitely film-like.

"You see, it showed me how *brave* you are. I shall never forget the sight of you tackling that villain while Theodosius" – her lovely lip curled scornfully – "just moaned and asked for raw beef. Just as if anyone was *likely* to be carrying raw beef about at a dance." She saw a large and impressive "close up" of her face as she went on soulfully: "You may not be *a* prince, Robert, but you're *my* prince."

"*Angel!*" responded Robert satisfactorily.

Chapter 2

William – the Great Actor

It was announced in the village that the Literary Society was going to give a play on Christmas Eve. It was tradition that a play should be given in the village every Christmas Eve. It did not much matter who gave it or what it was about or what it was in aid of, but the village had begun to expect a play of some sort on Christmas Eve. William's sister Ethel and her friends had at first decided to do scenes from *As You Like It*, but this had fallen through partly because Ethel had succumbed to influenza as soon as the cast was arranged, and partly because of other complications too involved to enter into.

So the Literary Society had stepped into the breach, and had announced that it was going to act a play in aid of its Cinematograph Fund. The Literary Society was trying to collect enough money to buy a cinematograph. Cinematographs, the President said, were so educational. But that was not the only reason. Membership of the Literary Society had lately begun to fall alarmingly, chiefly because, as everyone freely admitted, the meetings were so dull. They had heard Miss Greene-Joanes read her paper on "The Influence of Browning" five times, and they had had the Debate on "That the Romantic School has contributed more to Literature than the Classical School" three times, and they'd had a Sale of Work and a Treasure Hunt and a picnic and there didn't seem to be anything else to do in the literary line. Mrs Bruce Monkton-Bruce, the Secretary, said that it wasn't her fault. She'd written to ask Bernard Shaw, Arnold Bennett, E. Einstein, M. Coué and H. G. Wells to come down to address them and it wasn't her fault that they hadn't answered. She'd enclosed a stamped addressed envelope in each case. More than once they'd tried reading Shakespeare aloud, but it only seemed to send the members to sleep and then they woke up cross.

But the suggestion of the cinematograph had put fresh life into the Society. There had been nearly six new members (the sixth hadn't quite made up her mind) since the idea was first mooted. The more earnest ones had dreams of watching improving films, such as those depicting Sunrise on the Alps or the Life of a Kidney Bean from the cradle to the grave, while the less earnest ones considered that such films as the "Three Musketeers' and "Monsieur Beaucaire" were quite sufficiently improving. So far they had had a little "Bring and Buy Sale" in aid of it, and had raised five and elevenpence three farthings, but as Mrs Bruce Monkton-Bruce had said that was not nearly enough because they wanted a really good one.

The play was the suggestion of one of the new members, a Miss Gwladwyn. "That ought," she said optimistically, "to bring us in another pound or two."

The tradition of the Christmas Eve plays in the village included a silver collection at the door, but did not include tickets. It was rightly felt that if the village had to pay for its tickets, it would not come at all. The silver collection at the door, too, was not as lucrative as one would think because the village had no compunction at all about walking past the plate as if it did not see it even if it was held out right under its nose. It was felt generally that "a pound or two" was a rather too hopeful estimate. But still a pound, as Mrs Bruce Monkton-Bruce so unanswerably pointed out, was a pound, and anyway it would be good for the Literary Society to get up a play. It would, she said, with her incurable optimism, "draw them together." As a matter of fact, experience had frequently proved the acting of a play to have precisely the opposite effect . . . They held a meeting to discuss the nature of the play. There was an uneasy feeling that they ought to do one of Shakespeare's or Sheridan's, or, as Miss Formester put it, vaguely, "something of Shelley's or Keats'," but the more modest ones thought that though literary, they were not quite as literary as that, and the less modest ones, as represented by Mrs Bruce Monkton-Bruce, said quite boldly and openly that though those authors had doubtless suited their own generations, things had progressed since then. She added that she'd once tried to read "She Stoops to Conquer," and hadn't been able to see what people saw in it.

"Of course," admitted Miss Georgine Hemmersley, "the men characters will be the difficulty." (The membership of the Literary Society was entirely feminine.) "I have often thought that perhaps it would be a good thing to try to interest the men of the neighbourhood in our little society."

"I don't know," said Miss Featherstone doubtfully, thinking of those pleasant little meetings of the Literary Society, which were devoted to strong tea, iced cakes, and interchanges of local scandal. "I don't know. Look at it how you will as soon as you begin to have men in a thing, it

complicates it at once. I've often noticed it. There's something *restless* about men. And they aren't literary. It's no
good pretending they are."

The Society sighed and agreed.

"Of course it has its disadvantages at a time like this,"
went on Miss Featherstone, "not having any men, I mean,
because, of course, it means that we can't act any modern
plays. It means we have to fall back on plays of historical
times. I mean wigs and things."

"I know," said Miss Gwladwyn demurely, "a perfectly
sweet little historical play."

"What period is it, dear?" said Mrs Bruce Monkton-
Bruce.

"It's the costume period," said Miss Gwladwyn simply.
"You know. Wigs and ruffles and swords. Tudor. Or is it
Elizabethan? It's about the Civil War, anyway, and it's really
awfully sweet."

"What's the plot of it?" said the Literary Society with
interest.

"Well," said Miss Gwladwyn, "the heroine" (a certain
modest bashfulness in Miss Gwladwyn's mien at this moment
showed clearly that she expected to be the heroine), "the
heroine is engaged to a Roundhead, but she isn't really in
love with him. At least she thinks she is, but she isn't. And
a wonderful Cavalier comes to her house to take refuge in a
terrible storm, and she takes him in meaning to hand him
over to her *fiancé*, you know. Her father's a Roundhead, of
course, you see. And then she falls in love with him, with
the Cavalier, I mean, and hides him, and then the *fiancé*
finds him and she tells him that she doesn't love him, but she
loves the other. That's an awfully sweet scene. There's a
snow-storm. I've forgotten exactly how the snow-storm
comes in, but I know that there is one, and it's awfully

effective. You do it with tiny bits of paper dropped from above. It makes an awfully sweet scene. There are heaps of characters too," she went on eagerly, "we could *all* have quite good parts. There's a comic aunt and a comic uncle and awfully sweet parts for my – I mean her parents and quite a lot of servants with really *good* parts. There'd be parts and to spare for *everyone*. Some of us could even take two. It's an awfully sweet thing altogether."

Mrs Bruce Monkton-Bruce looked doubtful.

"Is it *literary* enough, do you think," she said uncertainly.

"Oh *yes*," said Miss Gwladwyn, earnestly. "It *must* be. If it's historical it *must* be literary, mustn't it? I mean, it *follows*, doesn't it?"

Apparently the majority of the Literary Society thought it did.

"Anyway," said Miss Gwladwyn brightly, "I'll get the book and we'll have a reading and then vote on it. All I can say is that I've *seen* it and I've seen a good many of Shakespeare's plays too, and I consider this a much sweeter thing than any of Shakespeare's, and if that doesn't prove that it's Literary I don't know what does."

Again the Society seemed to find the logic unassailable and the meeting broke up (after tea and iced cake, a verbatim account of what Mrs Jones said to Mrs Robinson when they'd quarrelled last week, and a detailed description of the doctor's wife's new hat), arranging to meet the next week and read Miss Gwladwyn's play.

"I *know* that you'll like it," was Miss Gwladwyn's final assurance as she took her leave. "It's such an awfully sweet little thing."

The meeting took place early the next week. Miss Gwladwyn opened it by artlessly suggesting that as she'd seen the play before she should read the heroine's part. It was generally felt that as she had introduced the play to them, this was only her due.

The first scene was read fairly briskly. It abounded, however, in such stage directions as "When door opens howling of wind is heard outside." "Crash of thunder without," and such remarks as: "Hark how the storm does rage tonight," and: "Hear the beating of the rain upon the window-panes." "Listen! Do you not hear the sound of horses' hoofs?"

At the end of the scene Miss Georgine Hemmersley (who was a notorious pessimist) remarked:

"It will be very difficult to get those noises made."

"Those who aren't on the stage must make them," said Miss Gwladwyn.

"But we're all on the stage in this scene," objected Miss Georgine Hemmersley.

"Then we must have a special person to make them," said Miss Gwladwyn.

Miss Georgine Hemmersley threw her eye over the stage directions.

"They'll be very difficult to make," she said, "especially the wind. How does one make the sound of wind?"

"A sort of whistle, I suppose," said Miss Gwladwyn doubtfully.

"Y-yes," said Miss Georgine Hemmersley, "but *how?* I mean, *I* couldn't do it, for instance."

At that moment William passed down the street outside.

William was whistling – not his usual piercing blast of a whistle, but a slow, mournful, meditative whistle. As a matter of fact he was not aware that he was whistling at all. His mind was occupied with a deep and apparently insoluble problem – the problem of how to obtain a new football with no money or credit at his disposal. Only such an optimist as William would have tackled the problem at all. But William walking down the street, hands in pockets, scowling gaze fixed on the ground mechanically and unconsciously emitting a tuneless monotonous undertone of a whistle, was convinced that there must be a solution of the problem if only he could think of it . . . If only he could think of it . . . He passed by Mrs Bruce Monkton-Bruce's open window and his whistle fell upon a sudden silence within.

"What's that?" said Mrs Bruce Monkton-Bruce.

Miss Georgine Hemmersley went to the window.

"It's just a boy," she said.

Miss Gwladwyn followed her.

"It's that rough-looking boy one sees about so much," she said.

Mrs Bruce Monkton-Bruce joined them at he window.

"It's William Brown," she said.

They stood at the open window while William, wholly unconscious of their regard, still grappling mentally with his insoluble problem, passed on his way. His faint tuneless strain floated back to them.

"It – it *does* sound like the wind," said Miss Gwladwyn.

On an impulse Mrs Bruce Monkton-Bruce put her head out of the window.

"William Brown!" she called sharply. "Come here."

William turned and scowled at her aggressively.

"I've not done nothin'," he said. "It wasn't *me* you saw chasin' your cat yesterday."

"Come in here, William," she said. "We want to ask you something."

William stood hesitating, not sure whether to obey or whether to show his contempt of her by continuing his thoughtful progress down the street.

"WILLIAM BROWN," MRS MONKTON-BRUCE CALLED
SHARPLY. "COME HERE!"

WILLIAM SCOWLED AGGRESSIVELY. "I'VE NOT DONE NOTHIN'," HE SAID.

They probably only wanted him in to make a fuss about something he'd not done. Well, not *meant* to do anyway: well, not worth making a fuss about anyway. On the other hand it might be something else and if he went on he'd never know what they'd wanted him for. His curiosity won the day.

Taking a piece of chewing-gum, which he had absently been carrying in his mouth, from his mouth to his pocket, he proceeded to hoist himself up to the window-sill whence he had been summoned.

"*Not* that way, William!" said Mrs Bruce Monkton-Bruce sternly. "Come in by the front door, please, in the usual way."

William lowered himself to the street again, put the chewing-gum back into his mouth, stood for a minute obviously wondering whether it was worth while to go in by the front door in the usual way, decided apparently that though it probably wasn't, still there was just a chance that it might be, then, very, very slowly (as if to prove his complete independence, despite his show of obedience), went round to the front door.

"You may open the door and come in," called Mrs Bruce Monkton-Bruce from the window, "and don't forget to wipe your feet."

William opened the door and came in. He wiped his feet with a commendable and very lengthy thoroughness (whose object was to keep them waiting for him as long as possible), transferred his chewing-gum from his mouth to his pocket again, carefully arranged his cap between the horns of the stuffed head of an antelope which was hanging on the wall, thought better of it and transferred it to the stuffed head of a fox, which was hanging on the opposite wall, gazed critically for a long time at a stuffed owl in a cage, absently broke off a piece of a fern that grew in a plant pot next to the hat-stand, and finally entered the drawing-room. He stood in the doorway facing them still scowling aggressively and scattering bits of fern upon the carpet. His mind went quickly over the more recent events of his career in order to account for the summons. He was already regretting having obeyed it. He decided to take the offensive. Fixing a stern and scowling gaze upon Miss Greene-Joanes, he said:

"When you saw me in your garden yesterday, I was jus' gettin' a ball of mine that'd gone over the wall into your garden. I was simply tryin' to save you trouble by goin' an' getting' it myself, 'stead of troublin' you goin' to the front door. An' that apple was one what I found lyin' under your tree an' I thought I'd pick it up for you jus' to help you tidy up the place 'cause it looks so untidy with apples lyin' about under the trees all over the place."

"William," said Mrs Bruce Monkton-Bruce, "we did not ask you to come in order to discuss your visit to Miss Greene-Joanes' garden—"

William turned his steely eyes upon her and pursued his policy of taking the offensive.

"Those stones you saw me throwin' at your tree," he said, "was jus' to kill grubs 'n' things what might be doin' it harm. I thought I'd help you keep your garden nice by throwin' stones at your tree to kill the grubs 'n' things on it for you 'cause they were eatin' away the bark or somethin'."

"We didn't bring you in to talk about that either, William," said Mrs Bruce Monkton-Bruce. Then clearing her throat, she said: "You were whistling as you went down the road, were you not?"

William's stern and freckled countenance expressed horror and amazement.

"*Well!*" he said. "*Well!* I bet I was hardly makin' any noise at all. 'Sides" – aggressively – "there's nothin' to stop folks jus' *whistlin*", is there? In the *street*. If they *want* to. I wasn't doin' you any *harm*, was I? Jus' *whistlin' in the street*. If you've gotta headache or anythin' an' don' want me to I won't not till I get into the nex' street where you won't hear me. Not now I know. You needn't've brought me *in* jus' to say that. If you'd jus' shouted it out of the window I'd 've heard all right. But I don't see you can blame me jus' for—"

Mrs Bruce Monkton-Bruce held out a hand feebly to stem the tide of his eloquence.

"It's not that, William," she said faintly. "Do stop talking for two minutes, and let me speak. We – we were *interested* in your whistle. Would you – would you kindly repeat it in here – just to let us hear again what it sounds like?"

William was proud of his whistle and flattered to be thus asked to perform in public. He paused a minute to gather his forces together, drew in his breath, then emitted a sound that would have done credit to a factory syren.

Miss Georgine Hemmersley screamed. Miss Gwladwyn, who was poised girlishly on the arm of her chair, lost her balance and fell on to the floor. Mrs Bruce Monkton-Bruce clapped her hands to her ears with a moan of agony and Miss Greene-Joanes lay back in her chair in a dead faint, from which, however, as no one took any notice of her, she quickly recovered. William immensely flattered by this reception of his performance, murmured modestly:

"I can do a better one still this way," and proceeded to put a finger into each corner of his mouth and to draw in his breath for another blast.

With great presence of mind, Mrs Bruce Monkton-Bruce managed to put her hand across his face just in time.

"No, William," she said brokenly, "not like that – not like that—"

"I warn you," said Miss Greene-Joanes, in a shrill trembling voice, "I shall have hysterics if he does it again. I've already fainted," she went on, in a reproachful voice, "but nobody noticed me. I won't be answerable for what happens to me if that boy stays in the room a minute longer."

"Send him away," moaned Miss Featherstone, "and let's *imagine* the wind."

"Let's leave it to chance," pleaded Miss Greene-Joanes. "I can't bear it again. There – there may be a *natural* wind that night. It's quite possible."

"William," said Mrs Bruce Monkton-Bruce weakly, "it was a gentle whistle we wanted to hear. A whistle like – like – like the wind in the distance. A *long* way in the distance, William."

William emitted a gentle, drawn-out, mournful whistle. It represented perfectly the distant moaning of the wind. His stricken audience recovered and gave a gasp of amazement and delight.

"That was *very* nice," said Mrs Bruce Monkton-Bruce.

William, cheered and flattered by her praise, said: "I'll do it a bit nearer than that now," and again gathered his forces for the effort.

"No, William," said Mrs Bruce Monkton-Bruce again stopping him just in time. "That's as near as we want. That's *just* what we want . . . Now, William, we are going to get up a little play, and during the play the wind is supposed to be heard right in the distance – a long, *long* way in the distance, William. The wind is supposed to be a *very* distant one indeed, William. Perhaps for a very great treat we'll let you make that wind, William."

William's mind worked quickly. The apparently insoluble problem was still with him. He saw a means, not to solve it indeed, but to make it a little less insoluble. Assuming his most sphinx-like expression he said unblushingly, unblinkingly:

"Well, of course – that'll take up a good deal of my time. I dunno *quite* as I can spare all that time."

They were amazed at his effrontery and at the same time his astounding and unexpected reluctance to accept the post of wind-maker increased the desirability of his whistle in their eyes.

"Of course, William," said Mrs Bruce Monkton-Bruce in cold reproach, "if you don't want to help in a good cause like this—" Wisely she kept the exact nature of the good cause vague.

"Oh, I don' mind *helpin'*," said Willim; "all I meant was that it'd probably be takin' up a good deal of my time when I might be doin' useful things for other people. F'r instance, I often pump up my uncle's motor tyres for him." William's face became so expressionless as to border on the imbecile as he added: "He always gives me sixpence for doing that."

There was a short silence and then Mrs Bruce Monkton-Bruce said with great dignity:

"We will, of course, be pleased to give you sixpence for being the wind and any other little noises that may come into the play, William."

"Thank you," said William, concealng his delight beneath a tone of calm indifference. Sixpence . . . it was something to start from. William was such an optimist that with the first sixpence the whole fund seemed suddenly to be assured to him . . . He could do something else for someone else and get another sixpence and that would be a shilling, and, well, if he kept on doing things for people for sixpence, he'd soon have enough money to buy the football. Optimistically he ignored the fact that most people expected him to do things for them for nothing . . .

It was arranged that William should attend the next reading of the play in order to be the wind and whatever other noises might be necessary and then William, transferring his chewing-gum from his pocket to his mouth and scattering bits of fern absently to mark his path as he went, disappeared into the hall, took his cap from the fox's head, pulled a face at the stuffed owl, then, seeming annoyed by its equanimity, pulled another, absently plucked off another spray of Mrs Bruce Monkton-Bruce' cherished fern, and made his devastating way into the street. His piercing and unharmonious whistle shattered the quiet of countless peaceful homes as he strode onwards, cheered and invigorated by his visit, looking forward with equal joy to his rôle as wind-maker and his possession of the sixpence that was to be the nucleus of his football fund.

The members of the Literary Society heaved sighs of relief as the sounds of his departure faded into the distance.

"Don't you think," said Miss Greene-Joanes pathetically, "that we could find a *quieter* type of boy."

"But it *was*," said Mrs Bruce Monkton-Bruce, "it *was* a *very* good imitation of the wind. I mean, of course, when he did it softly."

"But wouldn't a quieter type of boy do?" persisted Miss Greene-Joanes. "For instance. there's that dear little Cuthbert Montgomery."

"But he can't whistle," objected Mrs Bruce Monkton-Bruce. "I'm afraid that you'd always find that the quiet type of boy couldn't do such a good whistle."

So reluctantly the Literary Society decided to appoint William as the wind.

William put in an early appearance at the next rehearsal. It was in fact a little too early for Mrs Bruce Monkton-Bruce, at whose house it was held. He arrived half an hour before the time at which it was to begin and spent the half-hour sitting in her drawing-room cracking nuts and practising his whistle. Mrs Bruce Monkton-Bruce said that it gave her a headache that lasted for a week.

"William," she said sternly when she entered the drawing-room, "if you don't learn to do a *quiet* whistle we won't have you at all."

"*Wasn't* that quiet?" said William, surprised. "It seemed to me to be such a quiet sort of whistle that I'm surprised you heard it at all."

"Well, I *did*," she snapped, "and it's given me a headache, and don't do it any more."

"Sorry," said William succinctly, transferring his whole attention to his nuts.

Her tone had conveyed to him that his position as wind-maker was rather precarious, so when the other members of the cast arrived he made his wind whistle so low that they had to request him to do it a *leetle* – just a *very leetle* – louder. Even then it sounded very faint and far away. William had decided not to risk either his sixpence or his place in the cast by whistling too loudly at rehearsals. The actual performance of course would be quite a different matter. His gentle whistle endeared him to them. They unbent to him. He was turning out, Miss Featherstone confided to Miss Gwladwyn in a whisper, a nicer type of boy than she had feared he would at first. He had helpful suggestions too about the other noises. He knew how to make the sound of horses' hooves. You did it with a coconut. And he knew how to make thunder. You did it with a tin tray. And he could make revolver shots by letting off caps or squibs or something. Anyway, he could do it somehow . . . They thought that perhaps he'd better not try those things till nearer the time. He'd better confine himself to the wind – so he confined himself to the wind, a gentle, anaemic sort of wind which he despised in his heart, but which he felt was winning him the confidence of his new friends. They unbent to him more and more. He was rather annoyed that he was not to have the snow-storm. Miss Gwladwyn said that her nephew would manage the snow-storm. She said that her nephew was a dear little boy with beautiful manners, who she admitted regretfully could not whistle, and might not be able to manage the other noises, but would, she was sure, manage the snow-storm perfectly.

William went home fortified by their praise of his distant whistle and two buns given him by Mrs Bruce Monkton-Bruce. On the way he met Douglas and Henry and Ginger.

"Hello," they said, "where've you been?"

"I've been to a rehearsal," said William with his own inimitable swagger. "I'm actin' in a play."

They were as impressed as even William could wish them to be.

"What play?" demanded Ginger.

"One the Lit'ry Society's gettin' up," said William airily.

"What's it called?" said Douglas.

William did not know what it was called, so he said with an air of careless importance:

"That's a secret. I've not got to tell anyone that."

"Well, what are you actin' in it?" said Henry.

William's swagger increased.

"I'm the most important person in it," he said. "They jolly well couldn't do it at all without me."

"You the *hero*?" said Ginger incredulously.

"Um," admitted William. "That's what I am."

After all, he thought, surely in a play where you were continually hearing and talking about the wind, the wind might be referred to as the hero. Anyway, he soothed his conscience by telling it that as he was the only man in the piece, he *must* be the hero.

"They'll all women," he continued carefully, "so of course they had to get a man in from somewhere to be the hero."

The Outlaws were not quite convinced, and yet there was *something* about William's swagger . . .

"Well," said Ginger, "I s'pose if you're the hero you'll be havin' rehearsals with 'em?"

"Yes," said William. "Course *I* will!"

"All right," challenged Ginger. "Tell us where you're havin' the nex' one an' we'll *see*."

"At Mrs Bruce's nex' Tuesday afternoon at three," said William promptly.

"All *right*," said the Outlaws, "an' we'll jolly well *see*."

So next Tuesday at three o'clock they jolly well *saw*. Hidden in the bushes in Mrs Bruce Monkton-Bruce's (let us call her by her full name. She hated to hear it as she said "murdered") garden they saw the cast of "A Trial of Love" arrive one by one at the front door. And with them arrived William – the only male character – swaggering self-consciously but quite obviously as an invited guest up Mrs Bruce Monkton-Bruce's front drive. He was fully aware of the presence of his friends in the bushes, though he appeared not to notice them. His swagger as he walked in at the front door is indescribable.

The Outlaws crept away silently and deeply impressed. It was true. William must be the hero of the play. They were torn between envy of their leader and pride in him. Though all of them would have liked to be the hero of a play, still they could shine in William's reflected glory. Their walk as they went away from Mrs Bruce Monkton-Bruce's front gate reflected something of William's swagger. William was a hero in a play. Well, people'd have to treat them *all* a bit diff'rent after that.

The rehearsal was on the whole a great success. William, afraid that his friends might be listening at the window and not wishing them to guess the comparative insignificance of his rôle, reduced his whistle to a mere breath. Mrs Bruce Monkton-Bruce said encouragingly: "Just a *leetle* louder, William," but Miss Greene-Jones said hastily: "Well, perhaps it would be as well to keep it like that for rehearsals, dear, and to bring it out just a *leetle* bit louder on the night."

So William, still afraid that the Outlaws were crouched intently outside the window, kept it like that.

It was decided at the end that William need not attend all the rehearsals. The cast found his stare demoralising, and his habit of transferring his piece of chewing-gum (he'd had it for three weeks now) from his mouth to his pocket and from his pocket to his mouth disconcerting. Also he would at intervals take a nut from another pocket and crack it with much noise and facial contortion. He always made a very ostentatious show of collecting all the shells and putting them into yet another pocket, but Mrs Bruce Monkton-Bruce's horrified gaze watched a little heap of broken nut-shells steadily growing upon her precious carpet by William's feet. William himself fondly imagined that he was behaving in an exemplary way. He had even offered each of them one of his nuts and had been secretly much

relieved at their refusal. They could not, he thought, expect
him to offer them a chew of his chewing-gum . . . But
he was supremely bored and was not sorry when informed
that it would be best for them to rehearse the play without
wind and thunder till they were a little more accustomed
to it.

He was not summoned to another rehearsal for a fortnight.
The play was, as Miss Georgine Hemmersley said "taking
shape beautifully." Miss Georgine Hemmersley as a Cavalier
looked quite dashing, despite her forty-odd years, and Miss
Featherstone as the Roundhead looked also very fine,
though she too had passed her first youth. It was, however,
as she said, only fair that those who had been in the society
longest should have the best parts . . . Miss Gwladwyn, they
all agreed, made a sweetly pretty heroine.

William arrived with all his paraphernalia of coco-nuts and
squibs and tin tray, and, he considered, put up the best show
of all of them. True, the rest of the cast seemed a little
irritable. They kept saying: "*Quietly*, William." "William,
not so *loud*." "William, we can't hear ourselves speak."
"William, stop making that *deafening* noise. Well, there isn't
any wind now." At the end Miss Greene-Joanes, who had
seemed strangely excited all the time, burst out:

"Now, I've got some news for you all . . . William you
needn't stay." William began to make elaborate and protracted preparations for his departure, but, intensely curious,
lingered within earshot. "I didn't tell you before we began,
because I knew it would make you too excited to act. It did
me. You'll never *guess* who's staying in the village."

"*Who?*" chorused the cast breathlessly.

"Sir Giles Hampton."

The cast uttered screams of excitement. The Cavalier said,
"What for?" and the Roundhead said, "Who told you?" and

the comic aunt and uncle said simultaneously, "Good *heavens!*"

"He's had a nervous breakdown," said Miss Greene-Joanes, "and he's staying at the inn here because of the air, and he's supposed to be incognito, but of *course* people recognise him. As a matter of fact, he's telling people who he is because he's not *really* keen on being incognito. Actors never are really. They feel frightfully mad if people don't recognise them."

"What's he like to look at?" said the comic aunt breathlessly.

"Tall and important-looking and rather handsome with very bushy eyebrows."

"Do you think he'll *come?*" said all the cast simultaneously.

"I don't know but—William, *will* you go home and stop dropping nutshells on the carpet."

There was a silence while all the cast waited impatiently for William to take his leave. With great dignity William took it. He was annoyed at his unceremonious ejection. Thinking such a lot of themselves and their old play, and where would they be, he'd like to know, without the wind and the thunder and the horses' hooves and all the rest of it? . . . Treating the most important person in the play the way they treated him . . .

He walked down the road scowling morosely, absent-mindedly cracking nuts and scattering nutshells about him as he went . . . At the end of the road he collided with a tall man with bushy eyebrows.

"You should look where you're going, my little man," said the stranger.

"Come to that, so should you," remarked William, who was still feeling embittered.

The tall man blinked.

"Do you know who I am?" he said majestically.

"No," said William simply, "an' I bet you don't know who I am either."

"I am a very great actor," said the man.

"So'm I," said William promptly.

"So great," went on the man, "that when they want me to play a part they give me any money I choose to ask for it."

"I'm that sort too," said William, thrusting his hands deeply into his trouble pockets. "I asked for sixpence an' they gave it me straight off. It's goin' to a new football."

"And do you know why I'm here, my little man?" said the stranger.

"No," said William without much interest and added: "I'm here because I live here."

"I'm here," said the man, "because of my nerves. Acting has exhausted my vitality and impaired my nervous system. I'm an artist, and like most other artists am highly strung. Do you know that sometimes before I go on the stage I tremble from head to foot."

"I don't," said William coolly. "I never feel like that when I'm actin'."

"Ah!" smiled the man, "but I'm always the most important person in the plays I act in."

"S'm I," retorted William. "I'm like that. I'm the most important person in the play I'm in now."

"Would you like to see the programme of the play I've just been acting in in London?" continued the actor, taking a piece of paper out of his pocket.

William looked at it with interest. It contained a list of names in ordinary-sized print; then an "and" and then "Giles Hampton" in large letters.

"Yes," said William calmly, "that's the way my name's goin' to be printed in our play."

"What play is it?" said the man yielding at last to William's irresistible egotism.

"It's called 'The Trial of Love'," said William. "It's for my football an' their cinematograph."

"Ha-ha!" said the man. "And may – may – ah – distinguishing strangers come to it?"

"Yes," said William casually, "*anyone* can come to it. You've gotter pay at least. Everyone's gotter pay."

"Well, I must certainly come," said the distinguished stranger. "I must certainly come and see you play the hero."

The dress rehearsal was not an unqualified success, but as Miss Featherstone said, that was always a sign that the real performance would go off well. In all the most successful plays, she said, the dress rehearsal went off badly. William quite dispassionately considered them the worst-tempered set of people he'd ever come across in his life. They snapped at him if he so much as spoke. They said that his wind was far too loud, though it was in his opinion so faint and distant a breeze that it was hardly worth doing at all. They objected also to his thunder and his horses' hooves. They said quite untruly that they were deafening. A deep disgust with the whole proceedings was growing stronger and stronger in William's breast. He felt that it would serve them right if he washed his hands of the whole thing and refused to make any of their noises for them. The only reason why he did not do this was that he was afraid that if he did they'd find some one else to do it in his place. Moreover he was feeling worried about another matter. He was aware that he did not take in the play such an important part as he had given his

friends to understand. He had given them to understand that
he took the principal part and was on the stage all the time,
whereas, though he quite honestly considered that he took
the principal part, he wasn't on the stage at all. Then there
was that man with bushy eye-brows he'd met in the village.
He'd probably come, and William had quite given him to
understand that he had his name on the programme in big
letters and took a principal part . . .

"*Thunder*, William," said Miss Gwladwyn irritably, inter-
rupting his meditations. "Why don't you keep awake and
follow where we are!"

William emitted a piercing whistle.

"Not *wind*," she snapped. "*Thunder*."

William beat on his tin tray.

Miss Greene-Joanes groaned.

"That noise," she said, "goes right through and *through*
my head. I can't bear it!"

"Well thunder is loud," said William coldly. "It's nachrally
loud. I can't help thunder being' nachrally loud."

"Thunder more gently, William," commanded Mrs Bruce
Monkton-Bruce.

Just to annoy them William made an almost inaudible
rumble of thunder, but to his own great annoyance it didn't
annoy them at all. "That's better, William," they said; and
gloomily William returned to his meditation. He'd seen the
programme and had hardly been able to believe his eyes
when he saw that his name wasn't on it at all. They hadn't
even got his name down as the wind or the thunder or the
horses' hooves or anything . . . If it hadn't been for that
sixpence he'd certainly have chucked up the whole thing . . .

They'd got to the snow-storm now. The curtains were half
drawn across and in the narrow aperture appeared Miss
Gwladwyn, the heroine. It was a very complicated plot, but

at this stage of it she'd been turned out of her home by her cruel Roundhead father and was wandering in search of her lost Cavalier lover.

She said: "How cold it it! Heaven, wilt thou show me any pity?" and turned her face up to the sky, and tiny snowflakes began to fall upon her face. The tiny snow-flakes were tiny bits of paper dropped down through a tiny opening in the ceiling by her well-mannered little nephew. He did it very nicely. William did not pay much attention to it. He was beginning to consider the whole thing beneath his contempt.

It was the evening of the performance. The performers were making frenzied preparations behind the scenes. Mr Fleuster was to draw the curtain, Miss Featherstone's sister was to prompt, and William was to hand out programmes. Mr Fleuster has not come into this story before, but he had been trying to propose to Miss Gwladwyn for the last five years and had not yet been able to manage it. Both Miss Gwladwyn and Miss Gwladwyn's friends had given him ample opportunities, but opportunities only seemed to make him yet more bashful. When he had not an opportunity he longed to propose, and when an opportunity of proposing came he lost his head and didn't do it. Miss Gwladwyn had done everything a really nice woman can do; that is to say, she had done everything short of actually proposing herself. Her friends had arranged for him to draw the curtain in the hopes that it would bring matters to a head. Not that they really expected that it would. It would, of course, be a good opportunity, and as such would fill him with terror and dismay.

Mr Fleuster, large and perspiring, stood by the curtain, pretending not to see that Miss Gwladwyn was standing quite near him and that no one else was within earshot, and that it was an excellent opportunity.

William stood sphinx-like at the door distributing programmes. His cogitations had not been entirely profitless. He had devised means by which he hoped to vindicate his position as hero. For one thing he had laboriously printed out four special programmes which he held concealed beneath the ordinary programmes, and which were to be distributed to Ginger, Douglas, Henry, and the actor, if the actor should come. He had copied down the dramatis personæ from the ordinary programme, but at the end he had put an "and" and then in gigantic letters:

Wind	Shots	
Rain	And All	**William Brown**
Thunder	Other Noises	
Horses' Hooves		

Seeing Ginger coming he hastily got one of his homemade programmes out and assuming his blankest expression handed it to him.

"Good ole William," murmured Ginger as he took it.

Then Henry came, and Henry also was given one.

"Why aren't you changin' into your things?" said Henry.

"I don't *ackshully* come on to the stage," admitted William. "I'm the most important person in the play as you'll soon jolly well see, but I don't *ackshully* come on to the stage."

He was glad to have got that confession off his chest.

Then Douglas came. He handed the third of his privately printed programmes to Douglas with an air of impersonal officialism, as if he were too deeply occupied in his duties to be able to recognise his friends.

There was only one left. That was for the actor. If the actor came. William peered anxiously down the road. The room was full. It was time to begin.

"William Brown!" an exasperated voice hissed down the room. William swelled with importance. Everyone would know now that they couldn't begin without him. He continued to gaze anxiously down the road. There he was at last.

"William *Brown!*"

The actor was almost at the door. He carried a parcel under his arm.

"William Brown," said someone in the back row obligingly, "they want you."

"*William – Brown!*" hissed Mrs Bruce Monkton-Bruce's face, appearing frenzied and bodiless like the Cheshire cat between the curtains.

The actor entered the hall. William thrust his one remaining programme into his hand.

"Thought you were the hero," said the actor, gazing at him sardonically.

William met his sardonic gaze unblinkingly.

"So I am," he said promptly, "but the hero doesn't *always* come on to the stage. Not in the *newest* sort of plays, anyway." He pointed to the large-lettered part of this programme. "That's me," he said modestly. "All of it's me."

With this he hastened back behind the curtain, leaving the actor reading his programme at the end of the room.

He was received with acrimony by a nerve-racked cast.

"Keeping us all waiting all this time."

"Didn't you *hear* us calling?"

"It's nearly twenty-five to."

"It's all right," said William in a superior manner that maddened them still further. "You can begin now."

Miss Featherstone's sister took her prompt-book, Mr Fleuster seized the curtain-strings, the cast entered the stage, William took his seat behind, and the play began.

Now William's plans for making himself the central figure of the play did not stop with the programmes. He considered that the noises he had been allowed to make at the rehearsals had been pitifully inadequate, and he intended tonight to produce a storm more worthy of his powers. Who ever heard of the wind howling in a storm the way they'd made him howl all these weeks? He knew what the wind howling in a storm sounded like and he'd jolly well make it sound like that. There was his cue. Someone was saying.

"Hark how the storm rages. Canst hear the wind?"

At the ensuing sound the prompter dropped her book and the heroine lost her balance and brought down the property mantelpiece on to the top of her. William had put a finger into each corner of his mouth in order to aid nature in the rendering of the storm. The sound was even more piercing than he had expected it to be. *That*, thought William, complacently noticing the havoc it played with both audience and cast, was something like a wind. That would show 'em whether he was the hero of the play or not. With admirable presence of mind the cast pulled itself together and continued. William's next cue was the thunder.

"List," said the heroine, "how the thunder rages in the valley."

The thunder raged and continued to rage. For some minutes the cast remained silent and motionless – except for facial contortions expressive of horror and despair – waiting for the thunder to abate, but as it showed no signs of stopping they tried to proceed. It was, however, raging so violently that no one could hear a word, so they had to stop again.

At last even its maker tired of it and it died away. The play proceeded. Behind the scenes William smiled again to himself. *That* had been a jolly good bit of thunder. He'd really enjoyed that. And it would jolly well let them all know he was there even if he wasn't dressed up and on the stage like the others. His next cue was the horses' hooves, and William was feeling a little nervous about that. The sound of horses' hooves is made with a coco-nut, and though William had managed to take his coco-nut (purchased for him by Mrs Bruce Monkton-Bruce) about with him all the time the play was in rehearsal, he had as recently as last night succumbed to temptation and eaten it. He didn't quite know what to do about the horses' hooves. He hadn't dared to tell anyone about it. But still he thought he'd be able to manage it. Here it was coming now.

"Listen," Miss Gwladwyn was saying, "I hear the sound of horses' hooves."

Then in the silence came the sound of a tin tray being hit slowly, loudly, regularly. The audience gave a yell of laughter. William felt annoyed. He hadn't meant it to sound like that. It wasn't anything to laugh at, anyway. He showed his annoyance by another deafening and protracted thunderstorm.

When this had died away the play proceeded. William's part in that scene was officially over. But William did not wish to withdraw from the public eye. It occurred to him that in all probability the wind and the thunder still continued. Yes, somebody mentioned again that it was a wild night to be out in. Come to that, the war must be going on all over the place. He'd better throw a few squibs about and make a bit more wind and thunder. He set to work with commendable thoroughness.

At last the end of the scene came. Mr Fleuster drew the

curtains and chaos reigned. Most of the cast attacked William, but some of them were attacking each other, and quite a lot of them were attacking the prompter. They had on several occasions forgotten their words and not once had the prompter come to their rescue. On one occasion they had wandered on to Act II and stayed there a considerable time. The prompter's plea that she'd lost her place right at the very beginning and hadn't been able to find it again was not accepted as an excuse. Then Miss Hemmersley was annoyed with Miss Featherstone for giving her the wrong cues all the way through, and Miss Gwladwyn was annoyed with Miss Greene-Joanes for cutting into her monologue, and Miss Greene-Joanes was annoyed with Mrs Bruce Monkton-Bruce for standing just where she prevented the audience having a good view of her (Miss Greene-Joanes), and when they couldn't find anyone else to be annoyed with they turned on William. Fortunately for William, however, there was little time for recrimination, as already the audience was clamouring for the second scene. This was the snow-storm scene. Miss Gwladwyn had installed her beautifully-mannered nephew in the loft early in the evening with a box of chocolate creams to keep him quiet. Miss Gwladwyn went on to the stage. The other actors retired to the improvised green-room, there to continue their acrimonious disputes and mutual reproaches. The curtain was slightly drawn. Miss Gwladwyn went into the aperture and leapt into her pathetic monologue, and William behind the scenes relapsed into boredom. He was roused from it by Miss Gwladwyn's nephew who came down the steps of the loft carrying an empty chocolate box and looking green.

"William," he said, "will you do my thing for me? I'm going to be sick."

"All right," said William distantly. "What do you do?"

William, not having been chosen as the snow-storm, had never taken the slightest interest in the snow-storm scene.

"You just get the bucket in the corridor and take it up to the loft and empty it over her slowly when she turns up her face."

"A' right," said William with an air of graciousness, secretly not sorry to add the snow-storm to his repertoire. "A' right. I'll carry on. Don' you worry. You go home an' be sick."

It was not William's fault that someone had put the stage fireplace in the passage in such a position that it completely hid the bucket of torn-up paper and that the only bucket visible in the passage was the bucket of water thoughtfully placed there by Mrs Bruce Monkton-Bruce in case of fire. William looked about him, saw what was apparently the only bucket in the passage, took it up and went to the stairs leading into the loft. It was jolly heavy. Water! Crumbs! He hadn't realised it was water. He'd an idea that it was torn-up paper for snow, but probably they'd changed their minds at the last minute and thought they'd have rain instead. Or perhaps they'd only had paper for rehearsals, and had meant to have water for the real performance all along. Well, certainly it *was* a bit more exciting than paper. He took it very carefully up the stairs, then knelt over the little opening where he could see Miss Gwladwyn down below. He was only just in time. She was already saying:

"How cold it is! Heaven, will thou show me no pity?"

Then slowly and with a beautiful gesture of despair she raised her face towards the ceiling to receive full and square the entire contents of a bucket of water. William tried conscientiously to do it slowly, but it was a heavy bucket and he had to empty it all at once. He considered that he was rather clever in hitting her face so exactly. For a moment the

SLOWLY, WITH A BEAUTIFUL GESTURE OF DESPAIR, MISS
GWLADWYN LOOKED UPWARD AT THE CEILING – TO RECEIVE,
FULL AND SQUARE IN HER FACE, THE CONTENTS OF
WILLIAM'S BUCKET OF WATER.

audience enjoyed the spectacle of Miss Gwladwyn sitting on the floor, dripping wet and gasping and spluttering. Then Mr Fleuster had the presence of mind to draw the curtain. After which he deliberately walked across to the dripping, spluttering, gasping Miss Gwladwyn and asked her to marry him. For five years he'd been trying to propose to a dignified and very correctly dressed and mannered Miss Gwladwyn, and he'd never had the courage, but as son as he saw her gasping, spluttering, dripping on the floor like that he knew that now was the moment or never. And Miss Gwladwyn, still gasping, spluttering, dripping, said, "Yes."

Then the entire cast began to look for William. Somehow it never occurred to them to blame Miss Gwladwyn's guileless nephew. They knew by instinct who was responsible for the calamity. William, realising also by instinct that he had made a mistake, slipped out into the darkness.

He was stopped by a tall form that blocked his way.

"Ha!" said the tall man. "Going already? I realised, of course, the last scene must be the *grand finale*. I had meant to present this to you at the end, but pray accept it now."

He went away chuckling, and William found himself clasping the most magnificent football he had ever seen in his life.

And that was not all.

For the next day there arrived a magnificent cinematograph for the Literary Society, sent by Sir Giles Hampton with a little note telling them that their little play had completely cured his nervous breakdown, that it would be a precious memory to him all the rest of his life, and that he was going back to London cheered and invigorated.

And that was not all.

There arrived for William some weeks later a ticket for a box at a London theatre.

William went, accompanied by his mother.

He came back and told his friends about it.

He said he'd seen a play called *Macbeth*, but he didn't think much of it, and he could have made a better storm himself.

Chapter 3

William's Birthday

It was William's birthday, but, in spite of that, his spirit was gloomy and overcast. His birthday, in fact, seemed to contribute to his gloom instead of lightening it. For one thing, he hadn't got Jumble, his beloved mongrel, and a birthday without Jumble was, in William's eyes, a hollow mockery of a birthday.

Jumble had hurt his foot in a rabbit trap, and had been treated for it at home, till William's well-meaning but mistaken ministrations had caused the vet to advise Jumble's removal to his own establishment. William had indignantly protested.

"*Why*'s he got to go away? *Me?* I've been *curin'* him, I tell you. Well, a gipsy boy told me about that. He said, tie beech leaves round it. Well, he started chewin' off his bandage himself. I din' tell him to. Well, I wanted to try splints. I read in a book about how to put a dog's legs into splints. An' he *liked* it. He liked it better'n what he liked the bandage . . . Well, he'll prob'ly die now without me to look after him, an' it'll be your fault."

His fury increased when his visits to the vet's establishment were forbidden. The vet explained quite politely that

William's presence there was having a deleterious effect upon his nerves and business.

"I din' do any harm," said William indignantly. "I couldn't help upsettin' that jar of goldfishes an' I din' reely start those two dogs fightin'. I bet they'd done it even if I'd not been there. An' I din mean that white rat to get out of my pocket an' get 'em all excited. An' I din' bother him for food or anythin' when dinner-time came. I jus' ate dog biscuits an' ant eggs an' any stuff I found about."

William's family, however, was adamant. William was not to visit the veterinary surgeon's establishment again.

"All right, he'll die," said William with gloomy conviction, referring not to the vet, whose death would have left him unmoved, but to Jumble, "an' it'll be all your faults, an' I hope you'll always remember that you killed my dog."

So annoyed was he with them that, in order to punish them, he lost his voice. This, of course, alone, would have been a reward rather than a punishment, but he insisted on writing all he had to say (which was a lot) on a slate with a squeaky slate-pencil that went through everyone's head. They gave him paper and pencil, and he deliberately broke the point on the first word, and then returned to his squeaky slate-pencil to explain and apologise at agonising length. Finally, in despair, they sent over to the doctor for some medicine which proved so nauseous that William's voice returned.

This episode increased the tension between William and his family, and, when the question of his birthday celebration was broached, feeling was still high on both sides.

"I'd like a dog for my birthday present," said William.

"You've got a dog," said his mother.

"I shan't have when you an' that man have killed it between you," said William. "I've seen him stickin' his fingers down their throats fit to choke 'em, givin' 'em pills an' things. An' he puts on their bandages so tight that their calculations stop flowin' an' that's jus' the same as stranglin' 'em."

"Nonsense, William!"

"Then why'd he stop me goin' to see 'em?" went on William dramatically. "'Cause he knew that I saw he was killin' 'em, chokin' 'em with givin' 'em pills an' puttin' tight bandages on 'em stoppin' their calculations flowin'. I've a good mind to go to the police. He ought to be done something to by lor."

"You're talking a lot of nonsense, William."

"Anyway, I want a dog for my birthday present. I'm sick of not havin' a dog. I've not had a dog for nearly three days now. Well, even if he doesn't kill Jumble – an' he's tryin' jolly hard – an' what dog can live when he's bein' choked an' strangled all day for nearly three days – well, even if he doesn't kill him, I want another dog. I want two more dogs," he added shamelessly, knowing that his family wouldn't give him another dog, and feeling that if he were going to have a grievance against them, he might as well have it for two dogs as one.

"Nonsense! Of course you can't have another dog."

"I said two more dogs."

"Well, you can't have two more dogs."

"I'm going to give you a bottle of throat mixture for my present," said Ethel, who had suffered more than anyone through the squeaky slate-pencil because she had been deputed to attend on him.

William glared at her.

"Yes," he said darkly, "you needn't think I don't know that you're trying to kill me as well as Jumble. Poisonin' *me* an' chokin' an' stranglin' *him*."

"Would you like a party for your birthday, William?" said his mother, vaguely propitiating.

William considered this offer for a moment in silence. His mother's idea of giving a party consisted in asking back all the people who had asked him to their parties, and William knew from experience that it was impossible to move her from this attitude. He assembled in a mental review all the people who had asked him to their parties that year, and the result was a depressing one.

"I'd like a party," he said, "if you'll let me ask—" There followed a list of the more rowdy members of the juvenile male population of the neighbourhood. Mrs Brown paled.

"Oh, but William," she said, "they're so rough, and if we give a party at all we *must* have little Susie Chambers and Clarence Medlow and all the people who've asked you—"

"Then I won't have one," said William, "anyone'd think it was a funeral treat you were tryin' to give me, not a birthday treat. It's not my *funeral*."

"No, it's more likely to be ours," said Ethel. "I can still hear the noise of that slate-pencil."

"I don't see how you can when it's stopped," said William, the matter-of-fact. "You can't hear things that aren't there to hear. At least not if you're not balmy."

He was evidently going to elaborate this theme in relation to Ethel, but Mrs Brown stopped him with a hasty "That will do, William," and William returned to a mournful contemplation of his birthday.

"You can have Ginger and Henry and Douglas to tea," said his mother, but it appeared that William didn't want Ginger and Henry and Douglas to tea. He explained that she always stopped them playing any interesting games when they *did* come to tea, and he'd rather go out with them and play interesting games in the fields or woods than have them to tea and get stopped every time they started an interesting game.

"Well, anyway," he said at last, brightening, "I needn't go to the dancing-class on my birthday afternoon."

The dancing-class was at present the bane of William's life. He had been dismissed from one dancing-class some years ago as a hopeless subject, but Mrs Brown, in whose breast hope sprang eternal, had lately entered him for another that was held in a girls' school in the neighbourhood. It took place on Wednesday afternoon, William's half-holiday, and it was an ever-present and burning grievance to him. He was looking forward to his birthday chiefly because he took for granted that he would be given a holiday from the dancing-class. But it turned out that there, too, Fate was against him. Of course he must go to the dancing class, said Mrs Brown. It was only an hour, and it was a most expensive course, and she'd promised that he shouldn't miss a single lesson, because Mrs Beauchamp said that he was very slow and clumsy, and she really hadn't wanted to take him. William, stung by these personal reflections, indignantly retorted that he *wasn't* slow and clumsy, and, anyway, he *liked* being slow and clumsy. And as for her not wanting to take him, he bet she was jolly glad to get him and he could dance as well as any of them if he wanted to, but he didn't believe in dancing and he never had and he never would, and so he didn't see the sense of making him go to a dancing-class, especially on his birthday. He added sarcastically that he noticed anyway that *she* (meaning Mrs Brown) took jolly good care not to go to a dancing-class on *her* birthday.

Mrs Brown was quietly adamant. She was paying a guinea for the course, she said, and she'd promised that he shouldn't miss any of it.

To William, wallowing with a certain gloomy relish in his

ill-fortune, it seemed the worst that could possibly happen to him. But it wasn't. When he heard that Ethel's admirer, Mr Dewar, was coming to tea on his birthday, his indignation rose to boiling point.

"But it's my birthday," he protested. "I don't want *him* here on my birthday."

William had a more deeply-rooted objection to Mr Dewar than to any of Ethel's other admirers. Mr Dewar had an off-hand facetious manner, which William had disliked from his first meeting with him. But lately the dislike had deepened, till William's happiest dreams now took the form of shooting Mr Dewar through the heart with his bow and arrow, or impaling him on a fence with his penknife or handing him over to the imaginary wild beasts who obeyed William's slightest behest.

For in the very early days of their acquaintance Mr Dewar had once come upon William, dressed in his Red Indian suit, cooking an experimental mixture of treacle and lemonade in an old sardine tin over a smoking fire in the shrubbery, and since then he had never met William, without making some playful reference to the affair. "Here comes the great chief Wild Head. Hast thou yet finished yon pale face thou wast cooking, friend?"

Or he would refer to William as "the great chief Dark Ears," "the great chief Sans Soap" or "the great chief Black Collar." Or he would say with heavy sarcasm: "How the flames of thy fire leapt up to the sky, great Chief! I still feel the heat of it upon my face."

William did not consider his character of Indian Chief to be a subject for jesting, but his black looks, in Mr Dewar's eyes, only added to the fun.

And this hated creature was coming to tea on his birthday, and would probably insinuate himself so much into Ethel's good graces that he would be coming now every day afterwards to darken William's life by his insults.

"But, William," said his mother, "you wouldn't have a party or anyone to tea, so you can't complain."

"You don't want us all to go into a nunnery because it's your birthday, do you?" said Ethel.

William wasn't quite sure what a nunnery was, but it sounded vaguely like a "monkery," so he muttered bitterly, "You'd suit one all right," and went out of the room so that Ethel could not continue the conversation.

He awoke on the morning of his birthday, still in a mood of unmelting resentment. He dressed slowly and his thoughts were a sort of refrain of his grievances. A dancing-class and that man to tea on his birthday. On his *birthday*. A dancing-class and that man to tea on his *birthday*. A dancing-class and that man to *tea* on his birthday. A *dancing*-class. On his *birthday* . . .

He went downstairs morosely to receive his presents.

Ethel, of course, had not dared to give him a bottle of throat mixture. She would have liked to, because she still felt very strongly about the slate pencil, but she had learnt by experience that it was wiser not to embark upon a course of retaliation with William, because you never knew where it would lead you. So she had bought for him instead a notebook and pencil, which was as nearly an insult as she dared offer him. She assumed a very kindly expression as she presented it, and William's gloom of spirit deepened, because he had a suspicion that she meant it as an insult, and yet he wasn't sure, and it would be as galling to his pride to accept it with gratitude when she meant it as an insult, as it would be to accept it as an insult when she meant it kindly. He kept a suspicious eye upon her while he thanked her, but

she showed no signs of guilt. His mother's present to him
was a dozen new handkerchiefs with his initials upon each,
his father's a new leather pencil-case. William thanked them
with a manner of cynical aloofness of which he was rather
proud.

During morning school he took a gloomy satisfaction in
initiating one of his new handkerchiefs into its new life. In
the course of the morning it was used to staunch the blood
from William's nose after a fight in the playground, to wipe
the mud from William's knees after a fall in a puddle, to
mop up a pool of ink from William's desk, to swaddle the
white rat that William had brought to school with him, and
as a receptacle for the two pennyworth of Liquorice All
Sorts that had been Ginger's present to him. At the end of
the morning its eleven spotless brothers would have passed
it by unrecognised.

"Now, William," said his mother anxiously at lunch,
"you'll go to the dancing-class nicely this afternoon, won't
you?"

"I'll go the way I gen'rally go to things. I've only got one
way of goin' anywhere. I don't know whether it's nice or
not."

This brilliant repartee cheered him considerably, and he
felt that a life in which one could display such sarcasm and
wit was after all to a certain degree worth living. But still –
no Jumble. A dancing-class. That man to tea. Gloom closed
over him again. Mrs Brown was still looking at him
anxiously. She had an uneasy suspicion that he meant to
play truant from the dancing-class.

When she saw him in his hat and coat after lunch she said
again: "William, you *are* going to the dancing-class, aren't
you?"

William walked past her with a short laugh that was wild

and reckless and dare-devil and bitter and sardonic. It was, in short, a very good laugh, and he was proud of it.

Then he swaggered down the drive, and very ostentatiously turned off in the opposite direction to the direction of his dancing-class. The knowledge that his mother's anxiety had deepened at the sight of this, was balm to his sore spirit. He did not really intend to play truant from the dancing-class. The consequences would be unpleasant, and life was, he considered, quite complicated enough without adding that. He walked on slowly for some time with an elaborate swagger, and then turned and retraced his steps in the direction of the dancing-class with furtive swiftness. To do so he had to pass the gate of his home, but he meant to do this in the ditch so that his mother, who might be still anxiously watching the road for the reassuring sight of his return, should be denied the satisfaction of it.

He could not resist, however, peeping cautiously out of the ditch when he reached the gate, to see if she were watching for him. There was no sign of her at door or windows, but – there was something else that made William rise to his feet, his eyes and mouth wide open with amazement. There, tied to a tree in the drive near the front door, were two young collies, little more than pups. Two dogs. He'd asked his family for two dogs and here they were. Two dogs. He could hardly believe his eyes. He stared at them, and shook himself to make sure that he was awake. They were still there. They weren't part of a dream. His heart swelled with gratitude and affection for his family. How he had misjudged them! How terribly he'd misjudged them! Thinking they didn't care two pins about his birthday, and here they'd got him the two dogs he'd asked for as a surprise, without saying anything to him about it. Just put them there for him to find. His heart still swelling with love and gratitude, he went up the drive. As he went the church clock struck the hour. He'd only just be in time for the dancing-class now, even if he ran all the way. His mother had wanted him to be in time for the dancing-class, and the sight of the two dogs had touched his heart so deeply that he wanted to do something in return to please his mother. He'd hurry off to the dancing-class at once, and wait till he came back to thank them for the dogs. He was sure that his mother would rather he was in time for the dancing-class than that he went in now to thank her for the dogs.

He stooped down, undid the two leads from the tree, and ran off again down the drive, the two dogs leaping joyfully beside him. In the road he found the leads rather a nuisance. The two dogs ran in front of him and behind him, leapt up at him, circled round him, and finally tripped him up so that he fell sprawling full length upon the ground. When this had happened several times it occurred to him to take off their leads. They still leapt and gambolled joyfully about him as he ran, evidently recognising him as their new owner. One was slightly bigger and darker than the other, but both were very young and very lively and very lovable. Soon he grew out of breath, and began to walk. The collies began to walk, too, but had evidently preferred running. The smaller one began to direct his energies to burrowing in the ditches, and the larger one to squeeze his lithe young body through the hedge. Having squeezed it through the hedge, he found himself to his surprise in a field of sheep. He did not know that they were sheep. It was his first day in the country. He had only that morning left a London shop. But dim, wholly incomprehended, instincts began to stir in him. William, watching with mingled consternation and delight, saw him round up the sheep in the field, and begin to drive them pell-mell through the hedge into the road; then, hurrying, snapping, barking, drive them down the road towards William's house. On the way lay another field of sheep, separated by a hedge from the road. The collie plunged into this field, too, drove the occupants out into the road to join his first flock, and began to chivvy the whole jostling perturbed flock of them down the road towards William's house.

William stood and watched the proceeding. The delight it afforded him was tempered with apprehension. He had not forgotten the occasion when he had tried to train Jumble to be a sheep dog. He had learnt then that farmers objected to their sheep being rounded up and removed by strange dogs, however well it was done (and William had persisted at the time, and still persisted, that Jumble made a jolly fine sheep dog). William's mind worked quickly in a crisis. The white undulating company was already some way down the road. Impossible to bring them back. Still more impossible to separate them into their different flocks.

The collie had now made his way into a third field in search of recruits, while his main army waited for him meekly in the road. William hastily decided to dissociate himself from the proceedings entirely, to have been walking quietly to his dancing-class, and not to have noticed that one of the dogs had left him to collect sheep from all the neighbouring fields. Better to let one of his dogs go than risk losing both . . .

He hurried on to the dancing-class, occasionally turning round to throw a glance of fascinated horrow at the distant sea of sheep that was still surging down the road. At their rear was William's new pet, chivvying them with gusto, his tail arched proudly like a plume.

William reluctantly turned the corner that hid the wonderful sight from him, and walked up the drive of the girls' school where the dancing-class was held. Aware of a group

of little girls in dancing-frocks clustered at the downstairs
window, he assumed a manly swagger, and called out curt
commands to his attendant hound. ("Here, sir. To heel!
Down sir!") Near the front door he tied the collie to a tree
with the lead, and entered a room where a lot of little boys
– most of whom William disliked intensely – were brushing
their hair and washing their hands and changing their shoes.
William changed his shoes, studied his hair in the glass and
decided that it really didn't need brushing, wiped his hands
on his trousers to remove any removable dirt, and began to
scuffle with his less sedate fellow pupils.

At last a tinkly little bell rang, and they made their way to
the large room where the dancing-class was held. From an
opposite door was issuing a bevy of little girls, dressed in
fairy-like frills and furbelows with white socks and dancing-
shoes. Following them was an attendant army of mothers
and nurses, who had been divesting them of stockings or
gaiters and outdoor garments. William greeted as many of
these fairy-like beings as would condescend to look at him
with his most hideous grimace. The one he disliked most of
all (a haughty beauty with auburn curls) was given him as a
partner.

"*Need* I have William?" she pleaded pitifully. "He's so
awful."

"I'm not," said William indignantly. "I'm no more awful
than her."

"Have him for a few minutes, dear," said Mrs Beauchamp,
who was tall and majestic and almost incredibly sinuous,
"and then I'll let you have someone else."

The dancing-class proceeded on its normal course. William
glanced at the clock and sighed. Only five minutes gone. A
whole hour of it. The longest hour of the week. And on his

birthday. His *birthday*. Even the thought of his two new dogs did not quite wipe out that grievance.

"Please may I stop having William now? He's doing the steps all wrong."

William defended himself with spirit.

"I'm doin' 'em right. It's her what's doin' 'em wrong."

The smallest and meekest of the little girls was given to William as a partner, because it was felt that she would be too shy to protest. For some minutes she tried conscientiously to dance with William, then she said reproachfully:

"You seem to have such a lot of feet. I can't put mine down anywhere where yours aren't."

"I've only got two," he said distantly, "same as other people. When I've got mine down, you should find somewhere else to put yours."

"If I do you tread on them," said the little girl.

"Well, you can't expect me not to have feet, can you?" said William. "Seems to me that what you all want to dance with is someone without any feet at all. Seems to me the best way to do is for me to put mine down first, and then you look where mine aren't and put yours there."

They proceeded to dance on this system till Mrs Beauchamp stopped them, and gave William another partner – a little girl with untidy hair and a roguish smile. She was a partner more to William's liking, and the dance developed into a competition as to who could tread more often on the other's feet. The little girl was unexpectedly nimble at this, and performed a sort of *pas seul* upon William's dancing slippers. He strove to evade her, but she was too quick for him. It was, of course, a pastime unworthy of a famous Indian chief, but it was better than dancing. He unbent to her.

"*NEED* I HAVE WILLIAM?" SHE PLEADED PITIFULLY.
"HE'S SO *AWFUL*."

"I'M NOT," SAID WILLIAM INDIGNANTLY. "I'M NO
MORE AWFUL THAN HER."

"It's my birthday to-day and I've had two dogs given me."

"*Oo!* Lucky!"

"An' I've got one already, so that makes three. Three dogs I've got."

"Oo, I say! Have you got 'em here?"

"I only brought one. It's in the garden tied to a tree near the door."

"Oo, I'm goin' to look at it when we get round to the window!"

"Yes, you have a look. It's a jolly fine dog. I'm goin' to train it to be a huntin' dog. You know, train it to fetch in the wild animals I shoot. One of the others is a performin' dog and the other's a sheep dog. They're all jolly clever. One of them's with the vet now an' I don't know if he'll come out alive. They kill 'em as soon as look at 'em, vets do. Chokin' 'em and stranglin' 'em. I bet what I'll do is rescue him. I bet I can train 'em to hold the vet down while I rescue Jumble from him. I'm not afraid of anyone and neither are my dogs."

Mrs Beauchamp was watching his steps with a harassed frown, and it was evident that it was only a question of seconds before she interfered.

"Not of *her* or of anyone," said William, meaning Mrs Beauchamp. "Got you."

"No, you didn't," said the little girl, neatly withdrawing her foot from William's descending slipper and placing it firmly upon the top, "Got *you.*"

"Well, here's the window. Have a look at my dog," said William.

They edged to the window, and there the little girl halted, making a pretence of pulling up her socks. Then she glanced out with interest, and stood suddenly paralysed with horror, her mouth and eyes wide open. But almost immediately her vocal powers returned to her and she uttered a scream.

"*Look!*" she said. "Oh, *look!*"

They crowded to the window – little girls, little boys, nurses and mothers.

The collie had escaped from his lead, and found his way into the little girls' dressing-room. There he had collected the stockings, gaiters and navy-blue knickers that lay about on tables and desks, and brought them all out on to the lawn, where he was happily engaged in worrying them. Remnants of stockings and gaiters lay everywhere about him. He was tossing up into the air one leg of a pair of navy-blue knickers. Around him the air was thick with wool and fluff. Bits of ravelled stockings, chewed-up gaiters, with here and there a dismembered hat, lay about on the lawn in glorious confusion. He was having the time of his life.

After a moment's frozen horror the whole dancing-class – little girls, little boys, nurses, mothers and dancing-mistress – surged out on to the lawn. The collie saw them coming and leapt up playfully, a gaiter hanging out of one corner of his mouth, and a stocking out of the other. It occurred to everyone simultaneously that the first thing to do was to catch the collie, and take the gaiter and stocking from him. They bore down upon him in a crowd. He wagged his tail in delight. All these people coming to play with him! He entered into the spirit of the game at once, and leapt off to the shrubbery, shaking his head excitedly so that the gaiter and stocking waved wildly in the air. In and out of the trees, followed by all these jolly people who were playing with him, back to the lawn, round the house, through the rose garden. A glorious game! The best fun he'd had for weeks . . .

Meanwhile William was making his way quietly home-
ward. They'd say it was all his fault, of course, but he'd
learnt by experience that it was best to get as far as possible
and as quickly as possible away from the scene of a crime.
Delayed retribution never had the inspired frenzy of retribution exacted on the spot.

As he walked along the road, is brows drawn into a frown,
his hands plunged into his pockets, his lips were moving as
he argued with an invisible accuser.

 "Well, how could I help it? Well, you gave me them,
didn't you? Well, how could I know it was a dog like that?
It's not done any real harm either. Jus' a few stockings an'
things. Well, they can buy some more, can't they? They're
cheap enough, aren't they? Grudgin' the poor dog a bit of
fun! They don't mind paying as much as a pair of stockings
for a bit of fun for themselves, do they? Oh no! Then why
should they grudge the poor dog a bit of fun? That's all I
say. An' it wasn't *my* fault, was it? I never trained him to eat
stockings an' suchlike, did I? Well, I couldn't have, could I?
– seein' I'd only had him a few minutes. An' what
I say is—'

He turned the bend in the road that brought his own
house in sight, and there he stood as if turned suddenly to
stone. He'd forgotten the other dog. The front garden was a
sea of sheep. They covered drive, grass and flower beds.
They even stood on the steps that led to the front door. The
overflow filled the road outside. Behind them was the other
collie pup, his tail still waving triumphantly, running to and
fro, crowding them up still more closely, pursuing truants
and bringing them back to the fold. Having collected the
sheep, his instinct had told him to bring them to his master.
His master was, of course, the man who had brought him

from the shop, not the boy who had taken him for a walk. His master was in this house. He had brought the sheep to his master . . .

His master was, in fact, with Ethel in the drawing-room. Mrs Brown was out, and was not expected back till tea-time. Mr Dewar considered he was getting on very well with Ethel. He had not yet told her about the two collies he had brought for her. She'd said last week that she "adored" collies, and he'd decided to bring her a couple of them next week. He meant to introduce the subject quite carelessly when he'd reached the right stage of intimacy. He possessed the dramatic instinct and liked to produce his effects at the right moment. And so, when she told him that he seemed to understand her better than any other man she'd ever met (she said this to all her admirers in turn) he said to her quite casually:

"Oh! by the way, I forgot to mention it but I just bought a little present – or rather presents – for you this afternoon. They're in the drive."

Ethel's face lit up with pleasure and interest.

"Oh, how perfectly sweet of you," she said.

"Have a look at them and see if you like them," he said.

She walked over to the window. He remained in his arm-chair, watching the back of her Botticelli neck, lounging at his ease – the gracious, generous, all-providing male. She looked out. Sheep – hundreds and thousands of sheep – filled the drive, the lawn, the steps, the road outside.

"Well," said Mr Dewar casually, "do you like them?"

She raised a hand to her head.

"What are they for?" she said faintly.

"Pets," said Dewar.

"*Pets?*" she screamed. "I've nowhere to keep them. I've nothing to feed them on."

"Oh, they only want a few dog biscuits," said Mr Dewar. "*Dog* biscuits?"

Ethel stared at them wildly for another second, then collapsed on to the nearest chair in hysterics.

Mrs Brown had returned home before Ethel had emerged from her hysterics. Mrs Brown had had literally to fight her way to her front door through a tightly packed mass of

"WELL," SAID MR DEWAR, "LOVELY PETS, AREN'T THEY?"

ETHEL TURNED AND FACED HIM. "PETS!" SHE SCREAMED. "I'VE NOWHERE TO KEEP THEM."

sheep. If Ethel hadn't forestalled her she'd have had hysterics herself. Mr Dewar was wildly apologetic. He couldn't think what had happened. He couldn't think how the dogs had got loose. He couldn't think where the other dog was. He couldn't think where the sheep had come from. The other dog arrived at the same moment as a crowd of indignant farmers demanding their sheep. It still had a gaiter hanging out of one corner of its mouth and a stocking out of the other. It was curveting coquettishly. It wanted someone else to play with it. William was nowhere to be seen.

William came home about half an hour later. There were no signs of Mr Dewar, or of the dogs, or the sheep. Ethel and Mrs Brown were in the drawing-room.

"I shall never speak to him again," Ethel was saying. "I don't care whether it was his fault or not. I shall always connect him with that horrible moment when I looked out and saw – it was like a nightmare – nothing but sheep as far as you can see. I've told him never to come to the house again."

"I don't think he'd dare to when your father's seen the state the grass is in. It looks like a ploughed field. You can hardly see where the beds begin, and everything in them's broken and trodden down. I shouldn't be a bit surprised if your father didn't talk of suing him."

"As if I'd want hundreds of *sheep* like that," said Ethel, who was still feeling distraught, and confused what Mr Dewar had meant to do with what he had actually done. "*Pets* indeed!"

"And Mrs Beauchamp's just rung up about the other dog," went on Mrs Brown. "It evidently followed William to the dancing-class and tore up some stockings and things there. I don't see how she can blame us for that. She was really very rude about it. I don't think I shall let William go to any more of her dancing-classes."

William sat listening with an expressionless face, as if he didn't know what they were talking about, but his heart was singing within him. No more dancing-classes . . . that man never coming to the house any more. A glorious birthday – except for one thing, of course. But just then a housemaid came into the room.

"Please, 'm', it's the man from the vet with Master William's dog. He says he's quite all right now."

William leapt from the room, and he and Jumble fell upon each other ecstatically in the hall. The minute he saw Jumble, William knew that he could never have endured to have any other dog beside him.

"I'll take him for a little walk," he said; "I bet he wants one."

The joy of walking along the road again with his beloved Jumble at his heels was almost too great to be endured. He sauntered along, Jumble leaping up at him in tempestuous affection. His heart was full of creamy content.

He'd got Jumble back. That man was never coming to the house any more.

He wasn't going to any more dancing-classes.

It was the nicest birthday he'd ever had in his life.

Chapter 4

William and the White Elephants

"William," said Mrs Brown to her younger son, "as Robert will be away, I think it would be rather nice if you helped me at my stall at the Fête."

William's father at the head of the table groaned aloud.

"*Another* Fête," he said.

"My dear, it's *centuries* . . . *weeks* since we had one last," said his wife, "and this is the Conservative Fête – and quite different from all the others."

"What sort 'f a stall you goin' to have?" said William, who had received her invitation to help without enthusiasm.

"A White Elephant stall," said Mrs Brown.

William showed signs of animation.

"And where you goin' to gettem?" he said with interest.

"Oh, people will give them," said Mrs Brown vaguely.

"*Crumbs!*" said William, impressed.

"You must be very careful with them, William," said his father gravely, "they're delicate animals and must be given only the very best buns. Don't allow the people to feed them indiscriminately."

"Oh, no," said William with a swagger, "I bet I'll stop 'em doin' it that way if *I'm* lookin' after 'em."

"And be very careful when you're in charge of them. They're difficult beasts to handle."

"Oh, I'm not scared of any ole elephant," boasted William, then wonderingly after a minute's deep thought, "*white* uns, did you say?"

"Don't tease him, dear," said Mrs Brown, to her husband, and to William, "white elephants, dear, are things you don't need."

"I know," said William, "I know I don't need 'em but I s'pose some people do or you wun't be sellin' 'em."

With that he left the room.

He joined his friends the Outlaws in the old barn.

"There's goin' to be white elephants at the Fête," he announced carelessly, "and' I'm goin' to be lookin' after them."

"*White elephants!*" said Ginger impressed, "an' what they goin' to do?"

"Oh, walk about an' give people rides same as in the Zoo an' eat buns an' that sort of thing. I've gotter feed 'em."

"Never seen *white* uns before," said Henry.

"Haven't you," said William airily, "they're – they're same as black uns 'cept that they're white. They come from the cold places – same as polar bears. That's what turns 'em white – roamin' about in snow an' ice same as polar bears."

The Outlaws were impressed.

"When are they comin'?" they demanded.

William hesitated. His pride would not allow him to admit that he did not know.

"Oh . . . comin' by train jus' a bit before the Sale of Work

begins. I'm goin' to meet 'em an' bring 'em to the Sale of
Work. They're s'posed to be savage but I bet they won't try
on bein' savage with *me*," he added meaningly. "I bet I c'n
manage any ole *elephant*."

They gazed at him with deep respect.

"You'll let me *help* with 'em a bit, won't you?"

"William, can I help *feed* 'em?"

"William, can I have a ride free?"

"Well, I'll see," promised William largely, and with odious
imitation of grown-up phraseology, "I'll see when the time
comes."

The subsequent discovery of the real meaning of the term
White Elephant filled William with such disgust that he
announced that nothing would now induce him to attend the
Fête in any capacity whatsoever. The unconcern with which
this announcement was received by his family further
increased his disgust. The disappointment of the Outlaws at
the disappearance of that glorious vision of William and
themselves in sole charge of a herd of snowy mammals
caused them to sympathise with William rather than jeer at
him.

"If there isn't no white elephants," said William bitterly,
"then why did they say there was goin' to be some?"

Ginger kindly attempted to explain.

"You see that's the point, William – there *isn't* white
elephants."

"Then why did they say there was?" persisted William.
"Fancy callin' *rubbish* white elephants. If you're goin' to
have a stall of rubbish why don' they *say* they're goin' to
have a stall of rubbish 'stead of callin' it White Elephants?
Where's the *sense* of it? White elephants! An' all the time
it's broken old pots an' dull ole books an' stuff like that.
What's the *sense* of it . . . callin' it White Elephants!"

Ginger still tried to explain.

"You see there *isn't* any white elephants, William," he said.

"Well, why do they say there is?" said William finally. "Well, I'm jus' payin' 'em out by *not* helpin' – that's all."

But when the day of the Fête arrived William had relented. After all there was something thrilling about serving at a stall. He could pretend that it was his shop. He could feel gloriously important for the time being at any rate, taking in money and handing out change . . .

"I don't *mind* helpin' you a bit this afternoon, mother," he said at breakfast with the air of one who confers a great favour.

His mother considered.

"I almost think we have enough helpers, thank you, William," she said, "we don't want too many."

"Oh, do let William feed the white elephants and take them out for a walk," pleaded his father.

William glowered at him furiously.

"Of course," said his mother, "it's always useful to have someone to send on messages, so if you'll just *be* there, William, in case I need you . . . I daresay there'll be a few little odd jobs you could do."

"I'll sell the things for you if you like," said William graciously.

"Oh, no," said his mother hastily, 'I – I don't think you need do *that*, William, thank you."

William emitted a meaningful "Huh!" – a mixture of contempt and mystery and superiority and sardonic amusement.

His father rose and folded up his newspaper.

"Take plenty of buns, William, and mind they don't bite you," he said kindly.

The White Elephant stall contained the usual medley of battered household goods, unwanted Christmas presents, old clothes and derelict sports apparatus.

Mrs Brown stood, placid and serene, behind it. William stood at the side of it surveying it scornfully.

The other Outlaws who had no official positions were watching him from a distance. He had an uncomfortable suspicion that they were jeering at him, that they were comparing his insignificant and servile position as potential errand-goer at the corner of a stall of uninspiring oddments with his glorious dream of tending a flock of snow-white elephants. Pretending not to notice them he moved more to the centre of the stall, and placing one hand on his hip assumed an attitude of proprietorship and importance . . . They came nearer. Still pretending not to notice them he began to make a pretence of arranging the things on the stall . . .

His mother turned to him and said, "I won't be a second away, William, just keep an eye on things," and departed.

That was splendid. Beneath the (he hoped) admiring gaze of his friends he moved right to the centre of the stall and seemed almost visibly to swell to larger proportions.

A woman came up to the stall and examined a black coat lying across the corner of it.

"You can have that for a shilling," said William generously.

He looked at the Outlaws from the corner of his eye hoping that they noticed him left thus in sole charge, fixing prices, selling goods and generally directing affairs. The woman handed him a shilling and disappeared with the coat into the crowd.

William again struck the attitude of sole proprietor of the White Elephant stall.

Soon his mother returned and he moved to the side of the stall shedding something of his air of importance.

Then the Vicar's wife came up. She looked about the stall anxiously, then said to William's mother:

"I thought I'd put my coat down just here for a few minutes, dear. You haven't seen it, have you? I put it just here."

William's mother joined in the search.

Over William's face stole a look of blank horror.

"It – it can't have been *sold*, dear, can it?" said the Vicar's wife with a nervous laugh.

"Oh no," said Mrs Brown, "we've sold nothing. The sale's not really been opened yet . . . What sort of a coat was it?"

"A black one."

"Perhaps someone's just carried it in for you."

"I'll go and see," said the Vicar's wife.

William very quietly joined Ginger, Henry and Douglas who had watched the *dénouement* open-mouthed.

"*Well!*" said Ginger, "*now* you've been an' gone an' done it."

"Sellin' her *coat*," said Henry in a tone of shocked horror.

"An' she'll prob'ly wear it to church on Sunday an' she'll see it," said Douglas.

"Oh, shut up about it," said William who was feeling uneasy.

"Well I should think you oughter *do* something about it," said Henry virtuously.

"Well, what c'n I do?" said William irritably.

"You won't half catch it," contributed Douglas cheerfully, "they'll be sure to find out who did it. You won't half catch it."

"Tell you what," said Ginger, "let's go an' get it back." William brightened.

"How?" he said.

"Oh . . . sort of find out where she's took it an' get it back," said Ginger vaguely, his spirits rising at the thought of possible adventure, "ought to be quite easy . . . heaps more fun than hangin' round here anyway."

A cursory examination of the crowd who thronged the Vicarage garden revealed no black coat to the anxious Outlaws. William had been so intent upon asserting his own importance and upon impressing his watching friends that he had not noticed his customer at all. She had merely been a woman and he had an uneasy feeling that he would not recognise her again even if he were to meet her.

"I bet she's not here," said Ginger, "'course she's not here. She'll've taken her coat home jolly quick I bet. She'd

"IT – IT CAN'T HAVE BEEN SOLD, CAN IT?" SAID THE VICAR'S WIFE

be afraid of someone comin' an' sayin' it was a mistake. I bet she'll be clearin' off home pretty quick now – coat an' all."

The Outlaws went to the gate and looked up and down the road. The rest of the company were clustered round the

"OH, NO," SAID MRS BROWN. "THE SALE'S NOT REALLY
OPENED YET. WHAT SORT OF COAT WAS IT?"

lawn where the Member, who was opening the Fête, had
just got to the point where he was congratulating the stall
holders on the beautiful and artistic appearance of the stalls,
and wincing involuntarily whenever his gaze fell upon the
bilious expanse of green and mauve bunting.

"*There* she is," said Ginger suddenly, "*there* she is –
walkin' down the road in it – *cheek!*"

The figure of a woman wearing a black coat could be seen
a few hundred yards down the road. The Outlaws wasted no
further time in conversation but set off in pursuit. It was
only when they were practically upon her that they realised
the difficulty of confronting her and demanding the return of
the coat which she had, after all, acquired by the right of
purchase.

They slowed down.

"We – we'd better think out a plan," said William.

"We can watch where she lives anyway," said Ginger.

They followed their quarry more cautiously.

She went in at the gate of a small house.

The Outlaws clustered round the gate gazing at the front
door as it closed behind her.

"Well, we've got to get it back *some* way," said William
with an air of fierce determination.

"Let's jus' try askin' for it," said Ginger hopefully.

"All right," agreed William and added generously, "*you*
can do it."

"No," said Ginger firmly, "I've done my part s'gestin' it.
Someone else's gotter *do* it."

"Henry can do it," said William, still with his air of lavish
generosity.

"No," said that young gentleman firmly, even pugnaciously, "I'm jolly well *not* goin' to do it. You went an' sold
it an' you can jolly well go an' ask for it back."

William considered this in silence. They seemed quite firm
on the point. He foresaw that argument with them would be
useless.

He gave a scornful laugh.

"Huh!" he said. "Afraid! *That's* what you are. *Afraid.*

Huh . . . Well, I c'n tell you *one* person what's not afraid of
an' ole woman in an ole black coat an' that's me."

With that he swaggered up the path to the front door and
rang the bell violently. After that his courage failed, and but
for the critical and admiring audience clustered round the
gate he would certainly have turned to flee while yet there
was time . . . A maid opened the door. William cleared his
throat nervously and tried to express by his back and
shoulders (visible to the Outlaws) a proud and imperious
defiance and by his face (visible to the maid) an ingratiating
humility.

"Scuse me," he said with a politeness that was rather
overdone, "Scuse me . . . if it's not troublin' you too
much—"

"Now, then," said the girl sharply, "none of your sauce."

William in his nervousness redoubled his already exaggerated courtesy. He bared his teeth in a smile.

"Scuse me," he said, "but a lady's jus' come into this
house wearin' a white elephant—"

He was outraged to receive a sudden box on the ear
accompanied by a "Get out, you saucy little 'ound," and the
slamming of the front door in his face.

William rejoined his giggling friends, nursing his boxed
ear. He felt an annoyance which was divided impartially
between the girl who had boxed his ears and the Outlaws
who had giggled at it.

"Oh yes," he said aggrievedly, "'seasy to laugh, in't it.
'Snice an' easy to *laugh* . . . an' all of you afraid to go an'
then *laughin'* at the only one what's brave enough. You'd
laugh if it was *you*, wun't you? Oh yes!" He uttered his
famous snort of bitter sarcasm and contempt. "Oh yes . . .
you'd laugh *then*, wun't you? You'd laugh if it was *your* ear
what she'd nearly knocked off, *wun't* you? Lots of people've

died for less than that an' then I bet you'd get hung for murderers. Your brain's in the middle of your head joined on to your ear, an' she's nearly killed me shakin' my brain up like what she did. . . . Oh yes, 'seasy to *laugh* an' me nearly dead an' my brains all shook up."

"Did she hurt you *awful*, William?" said Ginger.

The sympathy in Ginger's voice mollified William.

"I sh'd jus' *think* so," he said. "Not that I *minded*," he added hastily, "I don't mind a little pain like that . . . I mean, I c'n stand any *amount* of pain – pain what would *kill* most folks . . . but," he looked again towards the house and uttered again his short sarcastic laugh, "p'raps she thinks she's got rid of me. Huh! P'raps she thinks they can go on stickin' to the ole black coat what they've stole. Well, they're not . . . let me kin'ly tell them . . . they're jolly well *not* . . . I – I bet I'm goin' right into the house to get it off them, so *there*!"

The physical attack perpetrated on William by the house-maid had stirred his blood and inspired him with a lust for revenge. He glared ferociously at the closed front door.

"I'll go'n have a try, shall I?" said Ginger, who shared with William a love of danger and a dislike of any sort of monotony.

"All right," said William, torn by a desire to see Ginger also fiercely assailed by the housemaid and a reluctance to having his glory as martyr shared by anyone else. "What'll you say to 'em?"

"Oh, I've got an idea," said Ginger with what William considered undue optimism and self-assurance, "well, if she bought it for a shillin' I bet she'll be glad to sell it for *more'n* a shilling, won't she? Stands to reason, dun't it?"

Ginger, imitating William's swagger (for Ginger, despite almost daily conflicts with him, secretly admired William immensely), walked up to the front door and knocked with an imperious bravado, also copied from William. The haughty housemaid opened the door.

"G'd afternoon," said Ginger with a courteous smile, "Scuse me, but will you kin'ly tell the lady what's jus' come in here wearin' a black coat that I'll give her one an' six for it an'—"

Ginger also received a box on the ear that sent him rolling halfway down the drive, and the door was slammed in his face. It was opened again immediately and the red angry face of the housemaid again glared out.

"Any more of it, you saucy little 'ounds," she said, "an' I'll send for the police."

Ginger rejoined the others nursing his ear and making what William thought was an altogether ridiculous fuss about it.

"She din't hit you *half*'s hard's what she hit me," said William.

"She did," said the aggrieved Ginger, "she hit harder . . . a jolly sight harder. She'd nachurally hit harder the second time. She'd be more in practice."

"No, she wun't," argued William, "she'd be more tired the second time. She'd used up all her strength on me."

"Well, anyway I saw yours an' I felt mine an' could *tell* that mine was harder. Well, gettem to look at our ears. I bet mine's redder than what yours is."

"P'raps it is," said William, "it nachurally would be because of mine bein' done first an' havin' time to get wore off. I bet mine's redder now than what yours will be when yours has had the same time to get wore off in as what mine has . . . an' let me kin'ly tell you I saw yours an' I felt mine an' I know that mine was a *jolly* sight harder 'n yours."

After a spirited quarrel which culminated in a scuffle

which culminated in an involuntary descent of both of them into the ditch, the matter was allowed to rest. Ginger had in secret been somewhat relieved at the housemaid's reception of his offer as he did not possess one-and-six and would have been at a loss had it been accepted.

An informal meeting was then held to consider their next step.

"I votes," said Douglas who was the one of the Outlaws least addicted to dangerous exploits, "I votes that we jus' go back to the Fête. We've done our best," he added unctuously, "an' if the ole coat's sold, well, it's jus' sold, P'raps she'll be able to get it back by goin' to a lawyer or to Parliament or somethin' like that."

But William, having once formed a purpose, did not lightly relinquish it.

"*You* can go back," he said scornfully, "I'm jolly well not goin' back without that ole coat."

"All right," said Douglas in a resigned tone of voice, "I'll stay an' help."

To Douglas's credit be it said that having uttered his exhortation to caution he was always content to follow the other Outlaws on their paths of lawlessness and hazard.

"Tell you what I'm goin' to do," said William suddenly, "I've *asked* for it polite an' if they won't give it me then it's *their* fault, in't it? Well I've *asked* for it polite an' they wun't give it me so now I'm jolly well goin' to *take* it."

"I'll go with you, William," volunteered Ginger.

"I think," said William, frowning and assuming his Commander-in-Chief air, "I'd better go on alone. But you jus' stay near an' then if I'm in *reel* danger – sort of danger of life or death – I'll shout an' you come in an' rescue me."

This was such a situation as the Outlaws loved. They had by this time quite lost sight of what they were rescuing and why they were rescuing it. The thrill of the rescue itself filled their entire horizon . . .

They went round to the side gate where they crouched in the bushes watching the redoubtable William as he crept Indian fashion with elaborate "registration" of cunning and secrecy across a small lawn up to a small open window. Breathlessly they watched him hoist himself up and swing his legs over the window sill. They saw his freckled face still wearing its frown of determination as he disappeared inside the room.

He had meant to make his way through the room to the hall where he hoped to find the black coat hanging and to be able to abstract it without interference and return at once to his waiting comrades. But things are seldom as simple as we hope they are going to be. No sooner had he found himself in the room than he heard voices approaching the door and with admirable presence of mind dived beneath the round table in the middle of the room, whose cloth just – but only just – concealed him from view.

The lady whom the Outlaws had followed down the road – now divested of the fateful black coat – entered the room followed by another gayer and more highly-coloured lady.

"A *black* coat, did you say?" said the first lady.

William, beneath the table, pricked up his ears.

"Yes, if you *can*, dear," said the highly-coloured lady, "if you'd be so good, dear. I only want it for tomorrow for the funeral. I think I told you, didn't I, dear? A removed cousin whom I hardly knew – a *very* removed cousin – but they've invited me and one likes to show oneself appreciative of these little attentions – not that I think he'll have left me a penny in his will and it certainly isn't worth while *buying* black but I *have* a black dress and if you *wouldn't* mind lending me a black coat."

"Certainly," said the first lady. "I can let you have one with pleasure. It's in the hall. It's one I've only just bought . . ."

William ground his teeth . . . So it *was* in the hall! If he'd only been a few minutes earlier . . .

They went into the hall and William gathered that the black coat was being displayed.

"Quite a bargain, wasn't it?" he heard the first lady say.

It was all he could do to repress a bitter and scornful "Huh!"

They returned – evidently with the coat.

"Thank you so much, dear," said the highly-coloured lady, "it's just what I wanted and *so* smart. What was it like at the Fête . . .?" she was trying on the coat and examining herself smilingly in the overmantel mirror. "I must say it *does* suit me."

"Oh, very dull," said the first lady. "I really came away before it was actually opened. Just got what I wanted and then came away. It all looked as if it was going to be *most* dull."

The highly-coloured lady sniffed and her complacency gave way to aggrievement. "I must say that I was a bit *hurt* that they didn't ask me to give an entertainment. I can't help feeling that it was a bit of a *slight*. People have so often told me that no function about here is complete without one of my entertainments and then not to ask me to entertain at the Conservative Fête . . . well, I call it *pointed*, and it points to one thing and one thing only in my eyes. It points to jealousy, and intrigue, and spitefulness, and underhand-edness, and cunning, and deceit on the part of some person or persons unknown – but, believe *me*, Mrs Bute, quite easily guessed at!"

The highly-coloured lady was evidently in the state known

as "working herself up." Suddenly William knew who she was. She must be Miss Poll. He remembered now hearing his mother say only yesterday, "That dreadful Poll woman wants to give an entertainment at the Fête and we're *determined* not to have her. She's so *vulgar*. She'd cheapen the whole thing . . ."

He peeped at her anxiously from behind his concealing table-cloth, then hastily withdrew.

"Of course," said Mrs Bute, who sounded bored and as if she'd heard it many times before, "of course, dear, but . . . the coat will do, will it?"

"Very nicely, thank you," said Miss Poll rather stiffly because she thought that Mrs Bute really ought to have been more sympathetic. "*Good* afternoon, dear."

"I'll wrap it up for you," said Mrs Bute.

There was silence while she wrapped it up, then Miss Poll said, "*Good* afternoon, dear" again and went into the hall and there followed the sound of the closing of the front door, then sounds as of the mistress of the house going upstairs. William retreated through his open window and rejoined Douglas and Henry at the gate. Ginger had vanished.

"Quick," he said, "*she's* got it."

The figure of Miss Poll carrying a large paper parcel could be seen walking down the road. "We've gotter follow *her*. She's got it now."

At this minute Ginger reappeared.

"She's got it," William explained to him.

"Yes, but there's another," said Ginger, pointing, "there's *another* black coat hangin' up in the hall. I've been round an' looked through a little window an' *seen* it . . . it's *there*."

William was for a moment nonplussed. Then he said: "Well, I bet the one she's took's the one, 'cause I heard her say wasn't it a bargain, an' it *was* a bargain too. Huh! I'm goin' after her."

"Well, I'm *not*," said Ginger. "I'm goin' to stop here an' get the other one."

"All right," said William, "you an' Douglas stay here an' Henry'n me'll go after the other an' I *bet* you ours is the right one."

So quite amicably the Outlaws divided forces. Ginger and Douglas remained concealed in the bushes by the gate of Mrs Bute's house, warily eyeing the windows, while William and Henry set off down the road after Miss Poll's rapidly vanishing figure.

William and Henry stood at Miss Poll's gate and held a hasty consultation. Their previous experience did not encourage them to go boldly to the front door and demand the black coat.

"Let's jus' go in an' steal it," said Henry cheerfully. "'S not hers really."

But William seemed averse to this.

"No," he said, "I bet that wouldn't come off. I bet she's the sort of woman that's always poppin' up jus' when you don' want her. No, I guess we've gotter think out a *plan*."

He thought deeply for a few minutes, then his face cleared and over it broke a light that betokened inspiration.

"I *know* what we'll do. It's a *jolly* good idea. I bet . . . well, anyway, you come in with me an' see."

Boldly William walked up to the front door and rang the bell. Apprehensively Henry followed him.

Miss Poll, wearing the black coat (for she had been trying it on and fancied herself in it so much that she had not been able to bring herself to take it off to answer the bell), opened the door.

William, his face devoid of any expression whatever, repeated monotonously as though it were a lesson:

"G'afternoon Miss Poll, please will you come to the Fête to give an entertainment."

Miss Poll went rather red and for one terrible minute William thought that she was going to attack him as the maid had done – but the moment passed. Miss Poll was simpering coyly.

"You – you've been sent on a message, I suppose, little boy?" then, relieving William's conscience of the difficult task of answering this question, she went on, "I *thought* there must be some mistake . . . Of course," she simpered again, then pouted, "*really* I'd be quite within my rights to refuse to go. It's most discourteous of them to send for me like this at such short notice but," she gave a triumphant little giggle, "I *knew* that *really* they couldn't get on without me. They didn't send a note by you, I suppose?"

"No," said William quite truthfully.

She pouted again.

"Well, *that* I think is rather rude, don't you? However," the pout merged again into the simper, "I wouldn't be so *cruel* as to punish them for that by staying away. I *knew* they'd want me in the end. But these things are always so shamefully organised, don't you think so?"

William cleared his throat and said that he did. Henry, in response to a violent nudge from William, cleared his throat and said that he did too. Miss Poll, encouraged by their sympathy, warmed to her subject.

"Instead of writing to engage me *months* ago they send a message like this at the last minute . . . What would they have done if I'd been out?"

Again William said he didn't know and again Henry, in

response to a nudge from William, said he didn't know either.

"Well, I mustn't keep the poor dears waiting," said Miss Poll brightly. "I'll be ready in a second. I've only to put my hat on."

Then Miss Poll underwent a short inward struggle which William watched breathlessly. Would she keep on the black coat or would she change it for another? Wild plans floated through William's head. He'd say would she please go in something black because the Vicar had died quite suddenly that morning or – or the Member had just been murdered or something like that . . . It was obvious that Miss Poll was torn between the joy of wearing a coat in which she considered herself to look "smarter" in than anything else she possessed and the impropriety of wearing for a festal occasion a garment borrowed for the obsequies of the very removed cousin. To William's relief the coat won the day and after buttoning up the collar to give it an even smarter appearance than it had before and putting on a smart hat with a very red feather, she joined them at the door.

"Now I'm ready, children," she said, at which William scowled ferociously and Henry winced, "they didn't say which of my repertoire" (Miss Poll pronounced it reppertwaw) "I was to bring with me, did they?"

And again William said "no" with a face devoid of expression and with perfect truth. And Henry said "No," too.

"As it's such short notice," she went on, "they really can't expect *anything* in the way of – well, of make-up or dress, can they?"

William said that they couldn't and Henry, being nudged again by William, confirmed the opinion . . .

"Though I wish you children could see me in my charwoman skit. I'm an artist in make-up . . . Now, can you imagine me looking *really* old and ugly?"

Henry quite innocently said "Yes" and on being nudged by William, changed it to "yes, please." Miss Poll looked at Henry as if she quite definitely disliked him and turned her attentions to William.

"You know, dear . . . I can make myself to look *really* old. You'd never believe it, would you? Now guess how old I am, really?"

Henry, not wishing to be left out of it, said with perfect good faith, "fifty" and William, with a vague idea of being tactful, said "forty". Miss Poll who looked, as a matter of fact, about forty-five, laughed shrilly.

"You children *will* have your joke," she said, "now I wonder what I'd better do for them to start with? You know, what makes me so *unique* as an entertainer, children – and if I'd wanted to be I'd be *famous* now on the London stage – is that I'm *entirely* independent of such artificial aids as mechanical musical instruments and books of words and such things. I depend upon the unaided efforts of my voice – and I've a perfect voice for humorous songs, you know, children – and my facial expression. Of course I've a *magnetic* personality . . . that's the secret of the whole thing . . ."

William was tense and stern and scowling. He wasn't thinking of Miss Poll's magnetic personality. He was thinking of Miss Poll's coat. The first step had been to lure Miss Poll to the Fête; the second and, he began to think, the harder, would be to detach the coat from Miss Poll's person.

"It's – it's sort of gettin' hot, i'n't it?" he said huskily.

"Yes, isn't it?" said Miss Poll pleasantly.

William's heart lightened. "Wun't you like to take your coat off?" he said persuasively. "I'll carry it for you."

But Miss Poll who considered, quite erroneously, that the coat made her look startlingly youthful and pretty, shook her head and clutched the coat tightly at her neck.

"No, certainly not," she said firmly.

William pondered his next line of argument.

"I thought," he suggested at last meekly, "I thought p'raps you *sing* better without your coat."

Henry, who felt that he was supporting William rather inadequately, said: "Yes, you sort of look as if you'd sing better without a coat."

"What nonsense!" said Miss Poll rather sharply, "I sing *perfectly* well in a coat."

Then William had an idea. He remembered an incident which had taken place about a month ago which had completely mystified him at the time, but which he had stored up for possible future use. Ethel had come home from a garden party in a state bordering on hysterics and had passionately destroyed a perfectly good hat which she had been wearing. The reason she gave for this extraordinary behaviour had been that Miss Weston had been wearing a hat *exactly* like it at the garden party (*"exactly* like it . . . I could have killed her and myself," Ethel had said hysterically). The reason had seemed to William wholly inadequate. He met boys every day of his life wearing headgear which was exactly identical with his and the sight failed to rouse him to hysterical fury. It was one of the many mysteries in which the behaviour of grown-up sisters was shrouded – not to be understood but possibly to be utilised. Now he looked Miss Poll up and down and said ruminatingly, "Funny!"

"What's funny?" said Miss Poll sharply.

"Oh, nothin'," said William apologetically, knowing full well that Miss Poll would now know no peace till she'd discovered the reason for his ejaculation and steady contemplation of her.

"Nonsense!" she said sharply, "you wouldn't say 'funny' like that unless there was some reason for it, I suppose. If I've got a smut on my nose or my hat's on crooked *say* so and don't stand there *looking* at me."

William's steady gaze was evidently getting upon Miss Poll's nerves.

"Nothin'," said William again vaguely, "only I've just remembered somethin'."

"*What* have you remembered?" snapped Miss Poll.

"Nothin' much," said William, "only I've jus' remembered that I saw someone at the Fête jus' before I came out to you, in a coat *exactly* like that one what you've got on."

There was a long silence and finally Miss Poll said: "It *is* a little hot, *dear*. You were quite right. If you would be so kind as to carry my coat—"

She took it off, revealing a dress that was very short and very diaphanous and very, very pink, folded up the coat so as to show only the lining and handed it to William. William, though retaining his sphinx-like expression, heaved a sigh of relief, and Henry dropped behind Miss Poll to turn a cart wheel expressive of triumph in the middle of the road. They had reached the gate of the Vicarage now. They were only just in time . . .

William meant to thrust the coat into the arms of the Vicar's wife and escape as quickly as he could, leaving Miss Poll (for whom he had already conceived a deep dislike) to her fate.

It happened that the Member's agent had with difficulty and with the help of great persuasive power and a megaphone, collected the majority of the attendants at the Fête

"I'VE JUS' REMEMBERED," SAID WILLIAM, "THAT I SAW
SOMEONE AT THE FÊTE IN A COAT EXACTLY LIKE THAT ONE
WHAT YOU'VE GOT ON."

into a large tent where the Member was to "say a few words"
on the political situation. Many of those who had had
experience of the Member's "few words" on other occasions
had tried to escape but the agent was a very determined
young man with an Oxford manner and an eagle eye, and in
the end he had hounded them all in. The Member was just
buying a raffle ticket for a nightdress case and being particu-
larly nice to the raffle ticket seller partly because she was
pretty and partly because she might have a vote (one could
never tell what age girls were nowadays). The agent was

hovering in the background ready to tell him that his
audience was awaiting him as soon as he'd finished being
nice to the pretty girl, and at the same time keeping a wary
eye on the door of the tent to see that no one escaped . . .
And then the *contretemps* happened. Miss Poll tripped airily
up to the door of the tent in her pink, pink frock, peeped in,
saw the serried ranks of an audience with a vacant place in
front of them, presumably for the entertainer, and skipping
lightly in with a "*So* sorry to have kept you all waiting,"
leapt at once into her first item – an imitation of a tipsy
landlady, an item that Miss Poll herself considered the cream
of her repertoire. The audience (a very heavy and respectable audience) gaped at her, dismayed and astounded. And
when a few minutes later the Member, calm and dignified
and full to overflowing of eloquence and statistics, having
exchanged the smile he had assumed while being nice to the
pretty raffle ticket seller for a look of responsibility and
capability, and having exchanged his raffle ticket for a neat
little sheaf of notes (typed and clipped together by the
ubiquitous agent), appeared at the door of the tent he found
Miss Gertie Poll prancing to and fro before his amazed
audience, her pink, pink skirts held very high, announcing
that she was Gilbert the filbert, the colonel of the nuts. The
agent, looking over his shoulder, grew pale, and loose-
jawed. The Member turned to him with dignity and a certain
amount of restraint.

"What's all this?" he demanded sternly.

The agent mopped his brow with an orange silk
handkerchief.

"I – I – I've no idea, sir," he gasped weakly.

"Please put a stop to it," said the Member and added
hastily, remembering that the tent was packed full of votes,
"without any unpleasantness, of course."

I have said that the agent was a capable young man with an Oxford manner, but it would have taken more than a dozen capable young men with Oxford manners to stop Miss Gertie Poll in full flow of her repertoire. She went on for over an hour. She merely smiled bewitchingly at the agent whenever he tried to stop her without any unpleasantness, and when the Member himself appeared like a *deux ex machina* to take command of the situation, she blew him a kiss and he hastily retired.

Meanwhile William, triumphantly bearing the black coat, made his way up to the Vicar's wife. He met Ginger and Douglas, also carrying a black coat and on the same mission.

"Bet you tuppence mine's the one," said Ginger.

"Bet you tuppence mine is," said William, "where'd you get yours?"

"We got it out of her hall," said Douglas cheerfully, "we jus' walked in an' got it an' no one saw us . . . I bet *ours* is the one."

"Well, come on an' see," said William, pushing his way up to the stall presided over by the Vicar's wife.

"Here's your coat, Mrs Marks," he said handing it to her, "it was sold by mistake off the rubbish stall but we've got it back for you – me an' Henry."

Before the Vicar's wife could answer a frantic messenger came up to her.

"What *shall* we do?" she moaned. "Miss Poll's entertaining the tent and the Member can't speak."

"Miss *Poll!*" gasped the Vicar's wife, "we never asked her."

"No, but she's *come* and she's singing all her *awful* songs and no one can stop her and the Member can't speak."

The Vicar's wife, still absently nursing the coat that William had thrust into her arm, stared in front of her.

"But – but how awful!" she murmured, "how *awful!*"

Then Ginger came up and thrust the second coat into her unprotesting arms.

"Your coat, Mrs Marks," he said politely, "what we sold by mistake off the rubbish stall. Me an' Douglas've got it back for you."

He made a grimace at William which William returned with interest.

They waited breathlessly to see which coat the Vicar's wife should claim as her own.

She looked down at her armful of coats as if she saw them for the first time.

"B-but," she said faintly, "I got that coat back. The woman who bought it thought there must be some mistake and brought it to me. These aren't my coats . . . I don't know anything about these coats."

Shrill strains of some strident music-hall ditty came from the tent. A second messenger came up.

"She won't stop," she sobbed, "and the Member's foaming at the mouth."

"Oh, dear," said the Vicar's wife, clutching her bundle of coats still more tightly to her. "Oh, dear, oh, *dear!*"

At that moment a woman pushed her way through the crowds up to the Vicar's wife. It was Mrs Bute.

"Brought it here, they did," she panted. "Where is it? *Thieves!* Came into my hall bold as brass an' *took* it! . . . *There* it is!" she glared suspiciously at the Vicar's wife, "what've *you* got it for . . . *my* coat . . . I'd like to know. I'd—" She tore it out of her arms and the other coat too fell to the ground. "My *other* coat!" she screamed, "*both* my coats! *Thieves* – that's what you all are! *Thieves!*"

"Where are those boys?" said the Vicar's wife very faintly. But "those boys" had gone. William, resisting the strong

temptation to go and enjoy the spectacle of the Member
foaming at the mouth, had hastily withdrawn his little band
to a safe distance.

They were found, of course, and brought back. They were
forced to give explanations. They were forced to apologise
to all concerned, even to Miss Poll (who forgave them
because she'd had such a perfectly *ripping* afternoon and her
little show gone off so *sweetly* and everyone been so *adorable*). They were sent home in disgrace . . . William was
despatched to bed on dry bread and water, but being quite
tired by the day's events and the bread happening to be new
and unlimited in quantity, William's manly spirit survived
the indignity.

And William's mother said the next day: "I *knew* what
would happen." (William's mother always said that she knew
it would happen after it had safely – or dangerously –
happened.) "I *knew* that if I let William come and help
everything would go wrong. It always does. Selling people's
coats and stealing people's coats and getting that awful
woman to come that we'd *sworn* we'd never have again and
stopping the Member speaking when he'd taken *ages* over
preparing his speech, and upsetting the whole thing – well,
if anyone had told me beforehand that one boy William's
size could upset a whole afternoon like that I simply
shouldn't have believed them."

And William's father said: "Well, I warned you, William.
I told you they were difficult beasts to manage. Of course, if
you lose control of a whole herd of white elephants like that
they're bound to do some damage."

And William said disgustedly: "I'm just *sick* of white
elephants and black coats. I'm going out to play Red
Indians."

Chapter 5

William's Busy Day

William and the Outlaws strode along the road engaged in a lusty but inharmonious outburst of Community singing. It was the first real day of spring. The buds were bursting, the birds were singing (more harmoniously than the Outlaws) and there was a fresh invigorating breeze. The Outlaws were going fishing. They held over their shoulders their home-made rods and they carried jam-jars with string handles. They were going to fish the stream in the valley. The jam-jars were to receive the minnows and other small water creatures which they might catch; but the Outlaws, despite all the lessons of experience, were still hopeful of catching one day a trout or even a salmon in the stream. They were quite certain, though they had never seen any, that mighty water beasts haunted the place.

"Under the big stones," said William, "why, I bet there's all sorts of things. There's room for great big fish right under the stones."

"Well, once we turned 'em over an' there weren't any," Douglas the literal reminded him.

William's faith, however, was not to be lightly shaken.

"Oh, they sort of dart about," he explained vaguely, "by

the time you've turned up one stone to see if they're there they've darted off to the next an' when you turn over the next they've darted back to the first without you seein' 'em, but they're there all the time really. I bet they are. An' I bet I catch a great big whopper – a salmon or somethin' – this afternoon."

"Huh!" said Ginger, "I'll give you sixpence if you catch a salmon."

"A' right," said William hopefully, "an' don't you forget. Don't start pretendin' you said tuppence same as you did about me seein' the water rat."

This started a heated argument which lasted till they reached what was known locally as the cave.

The cave lay just outside the village and was believed by some people to be natural and by others to be part of old excavations.

The Outlaws believed it to be the present haunt of smugglers. They believed that smugglers held nightly meetings there. The fact of its distance from the sea did not shake their faith in this theory. As William said, "I bet they have their meetin's here 'cause folk won't suspect 'em of bein' here. Folks keep on the lookout for 'em by the sea an' they trick 'em by comin' out here an' havin' their meetin's here where nobody's on the lookout for 'em."

For the hundredth time they explored the cave, hoping to find some proofs of the smugglers' visits in the shape of a forgotten bottle of rum or one of the lurid handkerchiefs which they knew to be the correct smuggler's headgear, or even a piece of paper containing a note of the smugglers' latest exploit or a map of the district. For the hundredth time they searched in vain and ended by gazing up at a small slit in the rock just above their heads. They had noticed it before but had not given it serious consideration. Now

William gazed at it frowningly and said, "I bet I could get through that and I bet that it leads down a passage an' that," his imagination as ever running away with him, "an' that at the end of a passage there's a big place where they hold their meetin's an' I bet they're there now – *all* of 'em – holdin' a meetin'."

He stood on tiptoe and put his ear to the aperture. "Yes," he said, "I b'lieve I can hear 'em talkin'."

"Oh, come on," said Douglas, who was not of an imaginative turn of mind. "I want to catch some minnows an' I bet there aren't any smugglers there, anyway."

William was annoyed by this interruption, but, arguing strenuously, proving the presence of smugglers in the cave to his own entire satisfaction, he led his band out of the cave and on to the high road again.

The subject of smugglers soon languished. They were passing a large barrack-like house which had been in the process of being built for the best part of a year. It was finished at last. Curtains now hung at the windows and there were signs of habitation – a line of clothes flapping in the breeze in the back garden and the fleeting glimpse of a woman at one of the windows. A very high wall surrounded the garden.

"Wonder what it is," said Henry speculatively, "looks to me like a prison."

"P'raps it's a lunatic asylum," said Ginger, "why's it got a high wall round it like that if it's not a lunatic asylum?"

Discussing the matter animatedly they wandered on to the stream.

"Now catch your salmon," challenged Ginger.

"All right. I bet I will," said William doggedly.

For a short time they fished in silence.

Then William gave a cry of triumph. His hook had caught something beneath one of the big stones.

"There!" he said, "I've got one. I *told* you so."

"Bet it's not a salmon," said Ginger but with a certain excitement in his voice.

"I bet it is," said William, "if it's not a salmon I – I—" with a suddden burst of inspiration, "I'll go through that hole in the cave – so there!"

He tugged harder.

His "catch" came out.

It was an old boot.

They escorted him back to the cave. The hole looked far too small for one of William's solid bulk. They stood below and stared at it speculatively.

"You've *got* to," said Ginger, "you said you would."

"Oh, all right," said William with a swagger which was far from expressing his real feelings, "I bet I can easy get through that little hole an' I bet I'll find a big place full of smugglers or smuggled stuff inside. Give me a shove . . . that's it . . . *Oo*," irritably, "don't shove so *hard* . . . You nearly pushed my head off my neck . . . Go on – go on . . . Oo, I say, I'm getting through quite easy . . . it's all dark . . . it's a sort of passage . . ." William had miraculously scraped himself through the small aperture. Two large boots was all of him which was now visible to the Outlaws. Those, too, disappeared, as William began to crawl down the passage. It was mercifully a little wider after the actual opening. His voice reached them faintly.

"It's all dark . . . it's like a little tunnel . . . I'm going right to the end to see what's there . . . well, anyway if that wasn't a salmon I bet there *are* salmons there and I bet I'll catch one too one of these days, and—"

His voice died away in the distance. They waited rather anxiously . . . They heard nothing and saw nothing more.

William seemed to have been completely swallowed up by the rock.

William slowly and painfully (for the aperture was so small that occasionally it grazed his back and head) travelled along what was little more than a fissure in the rock. The spirit of adventure was high in him. He was longing to come upon a cave full of swarthy men with coloured handkerchiefs tied round their heads and gold ear-rings, quaffing goblets of smuggled rum or unloading bales of smuggled silk. Occasionally he stopped and listened for the sound of deep-throated oaths or whispers or smugglers' songs. Once or twice he was almost sure he heard them. He crawled on and on and on and into a curtain of undergrowth and out into a field. He stopped and looked around him. He was in the field behind the cave. The curtain of undergrowth completely concealed the little hole from which he had emerged. He was partly relieved and partly disappointed. It was rather nice to be out in the open air again (the tunnel had had a very earthy taste); on the other hand he had hoped for more adventures than it had afforded. But he consoled himself by telling himself that they might still exist. He'd explore that passage more thoroughly some other time – there might be a passage opening off it leading to the smugglers' cave – and meantime it had given him quite a satisfactory thrill. He'd never really thought he could get through that little hole. And it had given him a secret. The knowledge that that little tunnel led out into the field was very thrilling. He looked around him again. Within a few yards from him was the wall surrounding the house about which they had just been making surmises. Was it a prison, or an asylum or – possibly – a Bolshevist headquarters? William looked at it curiously. He longed to know. He noticed a small door in the wall standing open. He went up to it and peeped inside. It gave on to a paved yard which was empty. The temptation was too strong for William. Very cautiously he entered. Still he couldn't see anyone about. A door – a kitchen door apparently – stood open. Still very cautiously William approached. He decided to say that he'd lost his way should anyone accost him. He was dimly aware that his appearance after his passage through the bowels of the earth was not such as to inspire confidence. Yet his curiosity and the suggestion of adventure which their surmises had thrown over the house was an irresistible magnet. Within the open door was a kitchen where a boy, about William's size and height and not unlike William, stood at a table wearing blue overalls and polishing silver.

They stared at each other. Then William said, "Hello."

The boy was evidently ready to be friendly. He replied, "Hello."

Again they stared at each other in silence. This time it was the boy who broke the silence.

"What've you come for?" he said in a tone of weary boredom. "You the butcher's boy or the baker's boy or somethin'? Only came in this mornin' so I don' know who's what yet. P'raps you're the milk boy?"

"No, I'm not," said William.

"Beggin'?" said the boy.

"No," said William.

But the boy's tone was friendly so William cautiously entered the kitchen and began to watch him. The boy was cleaning silver with a paste which he made by the highly interesting process of spitting into a powder. William watched, absorbed. He longed to assist.

"You live here?" he said ingratiatingly to the boy.

"Naw," said the boy laconically. "House-boy. Only came today," and added dispassionately, "Rotten place."

"Is it a prison?" said William with interest.

The boy seemed to resent the question.

"Prison yourself," he said with spirit.

"A lunatic asylum, then?" said William.

This seemed to sting the boy yet further.

"Garn," he said pugnaciously. "Oo're yer callin' a lunatic asylum?"

"I din' mean *you*," said William pacifically. "P'raps it's a place where they make plots."

The boy relapsed into boredom. "I dunno what they make," he said. "Only came this mornin'. *They've* gorn off to 'is *aunt* but the other one – *she's* still here, you bet, a-ringin' an' a-ringin' an' a-ringin' at her bell, an' givin' no one peace nowheres." He warmed to his theme. "I wouldn've come if I'd knowed. House-maid went off yesterday wivout notice. *She'd* 'ad as much as she wanted an' only the ole cook 'sides myself an' *her* upstairs a-ringin' an' a-ringin' at her bell an' givin' no one no peace nowheres an' the other two off to their aunt's. No place fit to call a place *I* don't call it." He spat viciously into his powder. "Yus, an' anyone can have my job."

"Can I?" said William eagerly.

During the last few minutes a longing to make paste by spitting into a powder and then to clean silver with it had grown in William's soul till it was a consuming passion.

The boy looked at him in surprise and suspicion, not sure whether the question was intended as an insult.

"What *you* doin' an' where *you* come from?" he demanded aggressively.

"Been fishin'," said William, "an' I jolly nearly caught a salmon."

The boy looked out of the window. It was still the first real day of spring.

"Crumbs!" he said enviously, *"fishin'."* He gazed with distaste at his work, "an' me muckin' about with this 'ere."

"Well," suggested William simply, "you go out an' fish an' I'll go on muckin' about with that."

The boy stared at him again first in amazement and finally with speculation.

"Yus," he said at last, "an' you pinch my screw. Not *much!*"

"No, I won't," said William with great emphasis. "I won't. Honest I won't. I'll give it to you. I don't want it. I only want," again he gazed enviously at the boy's engaging pastime, "I only want to clean silver same as you're doin'."

"Then there's the car to clean with the 'ose pipe."

William's eyes gleamed.

"I bet I can do that," he said, "an' what after that?"

"Dunno," said the boy, "that's all they told me. The ole cook'll tell you what to do next. I specks," optimistically, "she won't notice you not bein' me with only comin' this mornin' an' her run off her feet what with *her* ringin' her bell all the time an' givin' no one no peace an' *them* bein' away. Anyway," he ended defiantly, "I don't care if she does. It ain't the sort of place *I've* bin used to an' for two pins I'd tell 'em so."

He took a length of string from his pocket, a pin from a pincushion which hung by the fire-place, a jam jar from a cupboard, then looked uncertainly at William.

"I c'n find a stick down there by the stream," he said, "an' I won't stay long. I bet I'll be back before that ole cook comes down from *her* an' – well, you put these here on an' try'n look like me an' – I won't be long."

He slipped off his overalls and disappeared into the sunshine. William heard him run across the paved yard and close the door cautiously behind him. Then evidently he felt safe. There came the sound of his whistling as he ran across the field.

William put on the overalls and gave himself up to his enthralling task. It was every bit as thrilling as he'd thought it would be. He spat and mixed and rubbed and spat and mixed and rubbed in blissful absorption . . . He got the powder all over his face and hands and overalls. Then he heard the sound of someone coming downstairs. He bent his head low over his work. Out of the corner of his eye he saw a large hot-looking woman enter, wearing an apron and a print dress.

"Gosh!" she exclaimed as though in despair. "Gosh! of all the *places!*"

At that minute a bell rang loudly and with a groan she turned and went from the room again. William went on with his task of cleaning the silver. The novelty of the process was wearing off and he was beginning to feel rather tired of it. He amused himself by tracing patterns upon the surface of the silver with the paste he had manufactured. He took a lot of trouble making a funny face upon the teapot which fortunately had a plain surface.

Then the large woman came down again. She entered the kitchen groaning and saying "Oh, Lor!" and she was summoned upstairs again at once by an imperious peal of the bell. After a few minutes she came down again, still groaning and saying, "Oh, Lor!. . . First she wants hot milk an' then she wants cold milk an' then she wants beef tea an' then the Lord only knows what she wants . . . first one thing an' then another . . . I've fair had enough of it an' *them* goin' off to their aunt's an' that Ellen 'oppin' it an' *you* not much help to a body, are you?" she asked sarcastically. Then she looked at his face and screamed. "My Gosh! . . . What's 'appened to you?"

"Me?" said William blankly.

"Yes. Your face' as gone an' changed since jus' a few minutes ago. What's 'appened to it?"

"Nothin'," said William.

"Well, it's my nerves, then," she said shrilly. "I'm startin' seein' things wrong. An' no wonder . . . Well, I've 'ad enough of it, I 'ave, an' I'm goin' 'ome . . . *now* . . . first that Ellen 'oppin' it an' then *them* goin' off an' then '*er* badgerin' the life out of me. An' then your face changin' before me very eyes. Me nervous system's wore out, that's what it is, an' I've 'ad enough of it. When people's faces start changin' under me very eyes it shows I needs a change an' I'm goin' to 'ave one. That Ellen ain't the only one what can 'op it. '*Er* an' 'er bell-ringing – an' – an' *you* an' your face-chagin'! 'Taint no place for a respectable woman. *You* can 'ave a taste of waitin' on 'er an' you can tell *them* I've gone an' why – you an' your face!"

During this tirade she had divested herself of her apron and clothed herself in her coat and hat. She stood now and looked at William for a minute in scornful silence. Then her glance wandered to his operations.

"Ugh!" she said in disgust, "you nastly little messer, you! Call yourself a house-boy – changin' your face every minute. What d'you think you are? A blinkin' cornelian? An' messin' about like that. What d'you think you're doin'? Distemperin' the silver or cleanin' it?"

At this moment came another irascible peal at the bell.

"Listen!" said the fat woman. "Ark at 'er! Well, I'm orf. I'm fair finished, I am. An' you can go or stay *has* you please! Serve 'em right to come 'ome an' find us *hall* gone. Serve '*er* right if you went up to '*er* an' did a bit of face changin' at 'er just to scare 'er same as you did me. Do 'er good. Drat 'er – an' all of you."

She went out of the kitchen and slammed the back door. Then she went out of the paved yard and slammed the door. Then she went across the field and out of the field into the road and slammed the gate.

William stood and looked about him. A bell rang again with vicious intensity and he realised with mingled excitement and apprehension that he and the mysterious ringer were the only occupants of the house. The ringing went on and on and on.

William stood beneath the bell-dial and watched the blue disc waggle about with dispassionate interest. The little blue disc was labelled, "Miss Pilliter." Then he bethought himself of his next duty. It was cleaning the car with the hose. His spirits rose at the prospect.

The bell was still ringing wildly, furiously, hysterically, but its ringing did not trouble William. He went out into the yard to find the car. It was in the garage and just near it was a hose pipe.

William, much thrilled by this discovery, began to experiment with the hose pipe. He found a tap by which it could be turned off and on, by which it could be made to play fiercely or languidly. William experimented with this for some time. It was even more fascinating than the silver cleaning. There was a small leak near the nozzle which formed a little fountain. William cleaned the car by playing on to it wildly and at random, making enthralling water snakes and serpents by writhing the pipe to and fro. He deluged the car for about a quarter of an hour in a state of pure ecstasy . . . The bell could still be heard ringing in the house, but William heeded it not. He was engrossed heart and mind and soul in his manipulation of the hose pipe. At the end of the quarter of the hour he laid down the pipe and went to examine the car. He had performed his task rather too thoroughly. Not only was the car dripping outside; it was also dripping inside. There were pools of water on the floor at the back and in the front. There were pools on all the seats. Too late William realised that he should have tempered thoroughness with discretion. Still, he thought optimistically, it would dry in time. His gaze wandered round. It might be a good plan to clean the walls of the garage while he was about it. They looked pretty dirty.

He turned the hose on to them. That was almost more fascinating than cleaning the car. The water bounced back at you from the wall unexpectedly and delightfully. He could sluice it round and round the wall in patterns. He could make a mammoth fountain of it by pointing it straight at the ceiling. After some minutes of this enthralling occupation he turned his attention to the tap which regulated the flow and began to experiment with that. Laying the hose pipe flat on the floor he turned the tap in one direction till the flow was a mere trickle, then turned it in the other till it was a torrent. The torrent was more thrilling than the trickle but it was also more unmanageable. So he tried to turn the tap down again and found that he couldn't. It had stuck. He wrestled with it, but in vain. The torrent continued to discharge itself with unabated violence.

William was slightly dismayed by the discovery. He looked round for a hammer or some other implement to apply to the recalcitrant tap, but saw none. He decided to go back to the kitchen and look for one there. He dripped his way across to the kitchen and there looked about him. The bell was still ringing violently. The blue disc was still wobbling hysterically. It occurred to William suddenly that as sole staff of the house it was perhaps his duty to answer the bell. So he dripped his way upstairs. The blue disc had been marked 6. Outside the door marked six he stopped a minute, then opened the door and entered. A woman wearing an expression of suffering and a very purple dress lay moaning on the sofa. The continued ringing of the bell was explained by a large book which she had propped up against it in such a way as to keep the button pressed.

She opened her eyes and looked balefully at William.

"I've been ringing that bell," she said viciously, "for a whole hour without anyone coming to answer it. I've had three separate fits of hysterics. I feel so ill that I can't speak. I shall claim damages from Dr Morlan. Never, *never*, NEVER have I been treated like this before. Here I come – a quivering victim of nerves, *riddled* by neurasthenia – come here to be nursed back to health and strength by Dr Morlan, and first of all off he goes to some aunt or other, then off goes the housemaid. And I shall report that cook to Dr Morlan the minute he returns, the *minute* he returns. I'll sue for damages. I'll sue the whole lot of you for damages; I'm going to have hysterics again."

She had them, and William watched with calm interest and enjoyment. It was even more diverting than the silver cleaning and the hose pipe. When she'd finished she sat up and wiped her eyes.

"Why don't you *do* something?" she said irritably to William.

"All right – what?" said William obligingly, but rather sorry that the entertainment had come to an end.

"Fetch the cook," snapped the lady, "ask her how she *dare* ignore my bell for hours and *hours* and HOURS. Tell her I'm going to sue her for damages. Tell her—"

"She's gone," said William.

"*Gone!*" screamed the lady. "Gone where?"

"Gone off," said William; "she said she was fair finished an' went off."

"When's she coming back? I'm in a most critical state of health. All this neglect and confusion will be the *death* of my nervous system. When's she coming back?"

"Never," said William. "She's gone off for good. She said *her* nervous system was wore out an' went off – for good."

"Her nervous system indeed," said the lady, stung by the cook's presumption in having a nervous system. "What's anyone's nervous system compared with mine? Who's in charge of the staff, then?"

"Me," said William simply. "I'm all there is left of it."

He was rewarded by an even finer display of hysterics than the one before. He sat and watched this one, too, with critical enjoyment as one might watch a firework display or an exhibition of conjuring. His attitude seemed to irritate her. She recovered suddenly and launched into another tirade.

"Here I come," she said, "as paying guest to be nursed back to health and strength from a state of neurasthenic prostration, and find myself left to the mercies of a common house-boy, a nasty, common, low little rapscallion like you – find myself literally *murdered* by neglect, but I'll sue you for damages, the whole *lot* of you – the doctor and the housemaid and the cook and you – you nasty little – *monkey* . . . and I'll have you all hung for murder."

She burst into tears again and William continued to watch her, not at all stung by her reflections on his personal appearance and social standing. He was hoping that the sobbing would lead to another fit of hysterics. It didn't, however. She dried her tears suddenly and sat up.

"It's more than an hour and a half," she said pathetically, "since I had any nourishment at all. The effect on my nervous system will be serious. My nerves are in such a condition that I must have nourishment every hour, every hour at least. Go and get me a glass of milk at once, boy."

William obligingly went downstairs and looked for some milk. He couldn't find any. At last he came upon a bowl of some milky-looking liquid. Much relieved he filled a glass with it and took it upstairs to the golden-haired lady. She received it with a suffering expression and closing her eyes took a dainty sip. Then her suffering expression changed to one of fury and she flung the glass of liquid at William's head. It missed William's head and emptied itself over a Venus de Milo by the door, the glass, miraculously unbroken, encaging the beauty's head and shoulders. William watched this phenomenon with delight.

"You little fiend!" screamed the lady, "it's *starch!*"

"Starch," said William. "Fancy! An' it looked jus' like milk. But I say, it's funny about that glass stayin' on the stachoo like that. I bet you couldn't have done that if you'd tried!"

The lady had returned to her expression of patient suffering. She spoke with closed eyes and in a voice so faint that William could hardly hear it.

"I must have some nourishment at once. I've had nothing – *nothing* – since my breakfast at nine and now it's nearly eleven. And for my breakfast I only had a few eggs. Go and make me some cocoa at once . . . at once."

William went downstairs again and looked for some cocoa. He found a cupboard with various tins and in one tin he found a brown powder which might quite well be cocoa, though there was no label on it. Ever hopeful, he mixed some with water in a cup and took it up to the lady. Again she assumed her suffering expression, closed her eyes and sipped it daintily. Again her suffering expression changed to

one of fury, again she flung the cup at William and again she
missed him. This time the cup hit a bust of William Shakespeare. Though the impact broke the cup the bottom of it
rested hat-wise at a rakish angle upon the immortal bard's
head, giving him a rather debauched appearance while the
dark liquid streamed down his smug countenance.

"It's knife powder," screamed the lady hysterically. "Oh,
you murderous little *brute*. It's knife powder! This will be
the death of me. I'll never get over this as long as I live –
never, *never*, NEVER!"

William stood expectant, awaiting the inevitable attack of
hysterics. But it did not come. The lady's eyes had wandered
to the window and there they stayed, growing wider and
wider and rounder and rounder and wider, while her mouth
slowly opened to its fullest extent. She pointed with a
trembling hand.

"Look!" she said. "The river's flooding."

William looked. The part of the garden which could be
seen from the window was completely under water. Then –
and not till then – did William remember the hose pipe
which he had left playing at full force in the back yard. He
gazed in silent horror.

"I always *said* so," panted the lady hysterically, "I *said* so.
I said so to Dr Morlan. I said 'I couldn't live in a house in a
valley. There'd be floods and my nerves couldn't stand
them,' and he said that the river couldn't possibly flood this
house and it can and I might have known he was lying and
oh my poor nerves, what shall I do, what *shall* I do?"

William glanced around the room as if in search of
inspiration. He met the gaze of Venus de Milo soaked in
milk and leering through her enclosing glass; he met the
gaze of William Shakespeare soaked in water and knife

powder and wearing his broken cup jauntily. Neither afforded him inspiration.

"It rises as I watch it – inch by inch," shrilled the lady, "*inch* by *inch!* It's terrible . . . we're marooned . . . Oh, it's horrible. There isn't even a life belt in the house."

William was conscious of a great relief at her explanation of the spreading sheet of water. It would for the present at any rate divert guilt from him.

"Yes," he agreed looking out with her upon the water-covered garden. "That's what I bet it is – it's the river rising."

"Why didn't you *tell* me?" she screamed, "you must have known. Why, now I come to think of it, you were dripping wet when you first came into the room."

"Well," said William with a burst of inspiration, "I din' want to give you a sudden shock – what I thought it might give you tellin' you you was marooned—"

"Oh, don't *talk*," she said. "Go down at once and see if you can find any hope of rescue."

William went downstairs again. He waded out to the hose pipe and wrestled again with the tap beneath the gushing water. In vain. He waded into a neighbouring shed and found three or four panic-stricken hens. He captured two and took them up to the lady's room, flinging them in carelessly.

"Rescued 'em," he said with quiet pride, and then went down for the others. The mingled sounds of the squeaking and terrified flight of hens and the lady's screams pursued him down the stairs. He caught the other two hens and brought them up, too, carelessly flinging them in to join the chaos. Then he went down for further investigations. In another shed he found a puppy who had climbed into a box to escape the water and there was engaged in trying to catch a spider on the wall. William rescued the puppy, and took it upstairs to join the lady's menagerie.

"Rescued this, too," he said as he deposited it inside.

It promptly began to chase the hens. There ensued a scene of wild confusion as the hens, with piercing squawks, flew over chairs and tables, pursued by the puppy.

Even the lady seemed to feel that hysterics would have no chance of competing with this uproar, so she began to chase the puppy. William returned to the deluge in which he was

"HERE'S SOMETHIN' ELSE I'VE RESCUED," SAID WILLIAM PROUDLY.

beginning to find an irresistible fascination. He had read a story not long ago in which a flood figured largely and in which the hero had rescued children and animals from the passing torrent and had taken them to a place of safety at the top of a house. In William's mind the law of association was a strong one. As he gazed upon the surging stream he became the rescuer hero of the story and began to look round for something else to rescue. There appeared to be no more livestock to be rescued from the sheds. He waded

"PUT HIM DOWN HERE," MISS POLLITER SAID. "THIS IS
A NOBLE WORK, INDEED."

down to the road, which also was now partially under water, and looked up and down. A small pig had wandered out of a neighbouring farm and was standing contemplating the flooded road with interest and surprise. The hero rescuer of William's story had rescued a pig. Without a moment's hesitation William waded up to the pig, seized it firmly round the middle before it could escape, and staggered through the deluge with it and into the house. Though small it showed more resistance than William had expected. It wriggled and squeaked and kicked in all directions. Panting, William staggered upstairs with it. He flung open the door and deposited the pig on the threshold.

"Here's somethin' else I've rescued," he said proudly.

The lady was showing unexpected capabilities in dealing with the situation. She had taken the china out of the china cabinet and had put the hens into it. They were staring through the glass doors in stupid amazement and one of them had just complicated matters by laying an egg.

The lady was just disputing the possession of a table runner with the spirited puppy who thought she was having a game with it. The puppy had already completely dismembered a hassock, a mat and two cushions. Traces of them lay about the room. Venus and Shakespeare, still wearing their rakish head adornments, were gazing at the scene through runnels of starch and liquid knife-powder. Miss Polliter received the new refugee in a business-like fashion. She had evidently finally decided that this was no occasion for the display of nervous systems. She seemed, in fact, exhilarated and stimulated.

"Put him down here," she said. "That's quite right, my boy. Go and rescue anything else you can. This is a noble work, indeed."

The puppy charged the pig and the pig charged the china cabinet. There came the sound of the breaking of glass. The egg rolled out and the puppy fell upon it with wild delight. The hens began to fly about the room in panic again.

William hastily shut the door and went downstairs to continue his work of rescuing. He had by this time almost persuaded himself that the flood was of natural origin and that he was performing heroic deeds of valour in rescuing its victims. Again he looked up and down the road. He felt that he had done his duty by the animal creation and he would have welcomed a rescuable human being. Suddenly he saw two infants from the Infants School coming hand in hand down the road. They stared in amazement at the flood that barred their progress. Then with a touching faith in their power over the forces of nature, and an innate love of paddling, they walked serenely into the midst of the stream. When they reached the middle, however, panic overcame them. The smaller one sat down and roared and the larger one stood on tip-toe and screamed. William at once plunged into the stream and "rescued" them. They were stalwart infants but he managed to get one tucked under each arm and carried them roaring lustily and dripping copiously up to Miss Polliter's room. Again Miss Polliter had restored as if by magic a certain amount of order. She had cooped up the hens by an ingenious arrangement of the fireguard and she had put the pig in the coal-scuttle, leaving him an air-hole through which he was determinedly squeezing his snout as if in the hope of ultimately squeezing the rest of him. The puppy had dealt thoroughly with the table runner while Miss Polliter was engaged on the hens and pig, and was now seeing whether he could pull down window curtains or not.

William deposited his dripping, roaring infants.

"Some more I've rescued," he said succinctly.

Miss Polliter turned to him a face which was bright with interest and enterprise.

"Splendid, dear boy," she said happily, "splendid . . . I'll soon have them warmed and dried – or wait – is the flood rising?"

William said it was.

"Well, then, the best thing would be to go to the very top of the house where we shall be safer than here!"

Determinedly she picked up the infants, went out on to the landing and mounted the attic stairs. William followed holding the puppy who managed during the journey to tear off and (presumably – as they were never seen again) swallow his pocket flap and three buttons from his coat. Then Miss Polliter returned for the pig and William followed with a hen. The pig was very recalcitrant and Miss Polliter said "Naughty," to him quite sternly once or twice. Then they returned for the other hens. One hen escaped and in the intoxication of sudden liberty flew squawking loudly out of a skylight.

In the attic bedroom where Miss Polliter now assembled her little company of refugees she lit the gas fire and started her great task of organisation.

"I'll dry these dear children first," she said. "Now go down, dear boy, and see if there is anyone else in need of your aid."

William went downstairs slowly. Something of his rapture and excitement was leaving him. Cold reality was placing its icy grip upon his heart. He began to wonder what would happen to him when they discovered the nature and cause of his "flood," and whether the state to which the refugees were reducing the house would also be laid to his charge. He waded out to the hose pipe and had another fruitless struggle with the tap. Then he looked despondently up and down the road. The "flood" was spreading visibly, but there was no one in sight. He returned slowly and thoughtfully to Miss Polliter. Miss Polliter looked brisk and happy. She had apparently forgotten both her nervous system and its need of perpetual nourishment. She was having a game with the infants who were now partially dried and crowing with delight. She had managed to drive the hens into a corner of the room and had secured them there by a chest of drawers. She had tied the pig by a piece of string to the wash-hand-stand and it was now lying down quite placidly, engaged in eating the carpet. One hen had escaped from its "coop" and was running round a table pursued by or pursuing (it was impossible to say which) the puppy. Miss Polliter was playing pat-a-cake with the drying infants. She greeted William gaily.

"Don't look so sad, dear boy," she said. "I think that even though the river continues to rise all night we shall be safe here – quite safe here – and I daresay you can find something for these dear children to eat when they get hungry. I don't need anything. I'm quite all right. I can easily go without anything till morning. Now do one more thing for me, dear boy. Go down to my room on the lower floor and see the time. Dr Morlan said that he would be home by six."

Still more slowly, still more thoughtfully, William descended to her room on the lower floor and saw the time. It was five minutes to six. Dr Morlan might arrive then at any minute. William considered the situation from every angle. To depart now as unostentatiously as possible seemed to him a far, far better thing than to wait and face Dr Morlan's wrath. The hose pipe was damaged, the garden was flooded. Miss Polliter's room was like a battlefield after a battle, strange infants and a pig were disporting themselves about the house, a destructive puppy had wreaked its will upon every cushion and curtain and chair within reach (it had found that it could pull down window curtains).

William very quietly slipped out of the front door and crept down the drive. The flood seemed to be concentrating itself upon the back of the house. The front was still more or less dry. William crept across the field to the stile that led to the main road. Here his progress was barred by a group of three who stood talking by the stile. There was a tall pompous-looking man with a beard, a small woman and an elderly man.

"Oh, yes, we've quite settled in now," the tall, pompous-looking man was saying. "We've got a resident patient with us – a Miss Polliter who is a chronic nervous case. We are rather uneasy at having to leave her all to-day with only the cook and house-boy. Unfortunately our housemaid left us suddenly yesterday but we trust that things will have gone all right. An aunt of mine was reported to be seriously ill and we had to hurry to her to be in time but unfortunately – ahem – I mean fortunately – we found that she had taken a turn for the better so we returned as soon as we could."

"Of course," said the woman, "we'd have been back *ever* so much earlier if it hadn't been for that affair at the cave."

"Oh, yes," said the doctor, "very tragic affair, very tragic indeed. Some poor boy . . . there were a lot of people there trying to recover the body and they wanted to have a doctor in the unlikely case of the boy being still alive when they got him out. I assured them that it was very unlikely that he would be alive and that I had to get back to my own patient . . . and it would only be a matter of a few minutes to send for me . . . The poor mother was distraught."

"What had happened?" said the other man.

"Some rash child had crawled into an opening in the rock and had not come out. He must have been suffocated. His friends waited for over an hour before they notified the parents and I am afraid that it is too late now. They have repeatedly called to him but there is no response. As I told them, there are frequently poisonous gases in the fissures of the rock and the poor child must have succumbed to them. So far all attempts to recover the body have been unsuccessful. They have just sent for men with pickaxes."

William's heart was sinking lower and lower. Crumbs! He'd quite forgotten the cave part of it. Crumbs! He'd quite forgotten that he'd left the Outlaws in the cave waiting for him. The house-boy and the cook and the silver cleaning and the hose pipe and the flood and Miss Polliter and the hens and the pig and the puppy and the infants had completely driven the cave and the Outlaws out of his head. Crumbs, wouldn't everybody be mad!

For William had learnt by experience that with a strange perversity parents who had mourned their children as lost or dead are generally for some reason best known to themselves intensely irritated to find that they have been alive and well and near them all the time. William had little hopes of being received by his parents with the joy and affection that should be given to one miraculously restored to them from the fissures of the rock. And just as he stood pondering his next step the doctor turned and saw him. He stared at him for a few minutes, then said, "Do you want me, my boy? Anything wrong? You're the new house-boy, aren't you?"

William realised that he was still wearing the overalls which the house-boy had given him. He gaped at the doctor and blinked nervously, wondering whether it wouldn't be wiser to be the new house-boy as the doctor evidently thought he was. The doctor turned to his wife.

"Er – it *is* the new house-boy, dear, isn't it?" he said.

"I *think* so," said his wife doubtfully. "He only came this morning, you know, and Cook engaged him, and I hardly had time to look at him, but I think he is . . . Yes, he's wearing our overalls. What's your name, boy?"

William was on the point of saying "William Brown", then stopped himself. He mustn't be William Brown. William Brown was presumably lost in the bowels of the earth. And he didn't know the house-boy's name. So he gaped again and said:

"I don't know."

There came a gleam into the doctor's eye.

"What do you mean, my boy," he said. "Do you mean that you've lost your memory?"

"Yes," said William, relieved at the simplicity of the explanation, and the fact that it relieved him of all further responsibility. "Yes, I've lost my memory."

"Do you mean you don't remember anything?" said the doctor sharply.

"Yes," said William happily, "I don' remember anythin'."

"Not where you live or anything?"

"No," said William very firmly, "not where I live nor anything."

The other man, feeling evidently that he could contribute little illumination to the problem, moved on, leaving the doctor and his wife staring at William. They held a whispered consultation. Then the doctor turned to William and said suddenly:

"Frank Simpkins . . . does that suggest anything to you?"

"No," said William with perfect truth.

"Doesn't know his own name," whispered the doctor, then again sharply:

"Acacia Cottage . . . does that convey anything to you?"

"No," said William again with perfect truth.

The doctor turned to his wife.

"No memory of his name or home," he commented. "I've always wanted to study a case of this sort at close quarters. Now, my good boy, come back home with me."

But William didn't want to go back home with him. He didn't want to return to the house which still bore traces of his recent habitation and where his "flood" presumably still raged. He was just contemplating precipitate flight when a woman came hurrying along the road. The doctor's wife seemed to recognise her. She whispered to the doctor. The doctor turned to William.

"You know this woman, my boy, don't you?"

"No," said William, "I've never seen her before."

The doctor looked pleased. "Doesn't remember his own mother," he said to his wife: "quite an interesting case."

The woman approached them aggressively. The doctor stepped in front of William.

"Come after my boy," she said. "Sayin' 'is hour's ended at five an' then keepin' 'im till now! I'll 'ave the lor on you, I will. Where is 'e?"

"Prepare yourself, my good woman," said the doctor, "for a slight shock. Your son has temporarily – only temporarily, we trust – lost his memory."

She screamed.

"What've you bin doin' of to 'im?" she said indignantly, "'e 'adn't lorst it when 'e left 'ome this mornin'. Where is 'e, anyway?"

Silently the doctor stepped on to one side, revealing William.

"Here he is," he said pompously.

"'Im?" she shrilled. "Never seen 'im before."

They stared at each other for some seconds in silence. Then William saw the real house-boy coming along the road and spoke with the hopelessness of one who surrenders himself to Fate to do its worst with.

"Here he is."

The real original house-boy was stepping blithely down the road, an extemporised rod over his shoulder, swinging precariously a jar full of minnows. He was evidently ignorant of the flight of time. He saw William first and called out cheerfully:

"HERE IS YOUR SON," SAID THE DOCTOR POMPOUSLY.

"'IM?" SHRIEKED THE WOMAN, "NEVER SEED 'IM
BEFORE."

"I say, I've not been long, have I? Is it all right?"

Then he saw the others and the smile dropped from his face. His mother darted to him protectively.

"Oh, my pore, blessed child," she said, "what have they bin a-doin' to you – keepin' you hours an' hours after your time an' losin' your pore memory an' you your pore widowed mother's only child . . . Come home with your mother, then, an' she'll take care of you and we'll have the lor on them, we will."

The boy looked from one to another bewildered, then realising from his mother's tones that he had been badly treated he burst into tears and was led away by his consoling parent.

The doctor and his wife turned to William for an explanation. Their expressions showed considerably less friendliness than they had shown before. William looked about him desperately. Even escape seemed impossible. He felt that he would have welcomed any interruption. When, however, he saw Miss Polliter running towards them down the field he felt that he would have chosen some other interruption than that.

"Oh, there you are!" panted Miss Polliter. "Such *dreadful* things have happened. Oh, there's the dear boy. I don't know what we should have done without him . . . rescuing children and animals at the risk, I'm sure, of his own dear life. I must give you just a little present." She handed him a half-crown which William pocketed gratefully.

"But, my dear Miss Polliter," said the doctor, deeply concerned, "you should be resting in your room. You should never run like that in your state of nervous exhaustion . . . never."

"Oh, I'm quite well now," said Miss Polliter.

"Well?" said the doctor amazed and horrified at the idea.

"Oh, yes," said Miss Polliter, "I feel ever so well. The flood's cured me."

"The flood?" said the doctor still more amazed and still more horrified.

"Oh yes. The river's risen and the whole place is flooded out," said Miss Polliter excitely. "It's a most stimulating experience altogether. We've saved a lot of animals and two children."

The doctor was holding his head.

"Good Heavens!" he said. "Good Heavens! Good Heavens!"

At that moment two more women descended upon the group. They were the mothers of the infants. They had searched through the village for their missing offspring and at last an eye-witness had described their deliberate kidnapping and imprisonment in the doctor's house. They were demanding the return of their children. They were threatening legal proceedings. They were calling the doctor a murderer and a kidnapper, a vivisectioner, a Hun and a Bolshevist.

The doctor and the doctor's wife and Miss Polliter and the two mothers all began to talk at once. William, seizing his opportunity, crept away. He crept down the road towards the cave.

At the bend in the road he turned. The doctor and the doctor's wife and the two mothers and Miss Polliter, still all talking excitedly at the same time, began to make their way slowly up the hill to the doctor's house.

He looked in the other direction. There was a large crowd surrounding the cave; men were just coming along the road from the other direction with pickaxes to dig his dead body from the rock.

He went forward very reluctantly and slowly.

He went forward because he had a horrible suspicion that the doctor would soon have discovered the extent and the cause of the "flood" and would soon be pursuing him lusting for vengeance.

He went forward reluctantly and slowly because he did not foresee an enthusiastic welcome from his bereaved parents.

Ginger saw him first. Ginger gave a piercing yell and pointed down the road towards William's reluctant form.

"There – he *is!*" he shouted. "He's not dead."

They all turned and gaped at him open-mouthed.

William presented a strange figure. He seemed at first sight chiefly compounded of the two elements, earth and water.

He turned as if to flee but the figure of the doctor could be seen running down the road from his house after him; following the doctor were the doctor's wife, the infants' mothers with the infants and Miss Polliter. Even at that distance he could see that the doctor's face was purple with fury. Miss Polliter still looked bright and stimulated.

So William advanced slowly towards his gaping rescuers. "Here I am," he said. "I – I've got out all right."

He fingered the half-crown in his pocket as if it were an amulet against disaster.

He felt that he would soon need an amulet against disaster.

"Oh, where have you been?" sobbed his mother, "where *have* you been?"

"I got in a flood," said William, "an' then I lost my memory." He looked round at the doctor who was running towards them and added with a mixture of fatalistic resignation and bitterness, "Oh, well, he'll tell you about it. I bet you'll b'lieve him sooner than me an' I bet he'll make a different tale of it to what I would."

And he did.

But Miss Polliter (who left the doctor's charge, cured, to his great disgust, the next day) persisted to her dying day that the river had flooded and that the hose pipe had nothing to do with it.

And she sent William a pound note the next week in an envelope marked "For a brave boy".

And, as William remarked bitterly, he jolly well deserved it . . .

Chapter 6

Finding a School for William

William's suspicions were first aroused by the atmosphere of secrecy that enveloped the visit of Mr Cranthorpe-Cranborough. Mr Cranthorpe-Cranborough was a very distant cousin of William's father (so many times removed as to be almost out of sight) and was coming to stay for a weekend with the Browns. William gathered that his father had not met Mr Cranthorpe-Cranborough before in spite of the relationship, that the visitor was self-invited, and that the visit was in some way connected with himself. He gathered this last fact from whispered confabulations between his family during which they watched him in that way in which whispering confabulators always watch those who are the subject of the whispered confabulations.

William, while keeping eyes and ears alert, pretended to be sublimely unaware of all this. He went his way with an air of unsuspecting innocence that lured his family into a false security. "Fortunately," his mother whispered very audibly to Ethel once as he was just going out of the room, "William hasn't the slightest idea what he's coming for."

Meanwhile beneath William's exaggerated air of guileless-ness William's mind worked fast. Whenever he came upon any scattered twos he put them together to make four. These fours he stored up in mind as he went his way, apparently absorbed in his games, the well-being of his mongrel Jumble, the progress of his tamed caterpillars and earwigs, the shooting properties of his new bow and arrows, and the activities of his friends the Outlaws. But there was no look or sign or whisper from the grown-up world around him that the seemingly unconscious William did not intercept and store up for future reference. William, as some people had been known to put it, was "deep".

"Yes, dear," said Mrs Brown to Ethel, her nineteen-year-old daughter, "he's going to arrive before tea and your father's going to try to get home for tea, and they're going to talk it over together quietly after tea in the morning-room."

"Oh, well, I shall be busy," said Ethel, "I shall be helping Moyna Greene with her dress for the fancy dress ball, so I shan't be in their way. She's going as a lady of Elizabethan times and she's going to look *sweet*."

"I expect they'd like to be left alone to talk things over . . . Sh!" as she perceived William who had heard every word lolling negligently in the doorway cracking nuts.

"Well, William," brightly, "had a nice afternoon?"

"Yes, thanks," said William.

"We were just talking about Ethel's friend, Miss Greene, who's going to a fancy dress ball."

"Yes, I heard you," said William.

"She's going as a lady of the fourteenth century," proceeded Mrs Brown still brightly.

"Uh – huh," said William without interest as he cracked another nut.

Some of Mrs Brown's brightness faded.

"*William*!" she said indignantly, "*do* stop dropping shells on to the carpet."

"A'right – sorry," said William, stolidly turning to go away and cracking another nut.

"His *manners!*" said Ethel, elevating her small and pretty nose in disgust.

"Yes, dear," said Mrs Brown soothingly, "but *we* needn't bother about them *now*."

William wandered out into the garden. Though he did not for a minute cease his consumption of nuts he grew yet more thoughtful. He was beginning to look forward to the projected visit of Mr Cranthorpe-Cranborough with distinct apprehension. Whatever it boded, William felt sure that it boded no good to him. Still cracking nuts with undiminished energy and leaving a little trail of broken shells to mark his track over the immaculate lawn (and incidentally to make the gardener rise to dazzling heights of eloquence when he tried to mow it the next morning) William withdrew to the strip of untended shrubbery at the bottom of the garden, and, sitting down upon a laurel bush, began thoughtfully to throw pebbles at the next door cat who was its only other occupant. The next door cat, who looked upon William's pebble-throwing as a sign of his affection, began to purr loudly . . .

William considered the situation. This Mr Cranthorpe-Cranborough was coming for some sinister purpose tomorrow. That sinister purpose must at all costs be frustrated. But first of all he must find out what that sinister purpose was . . . He threw another handful of nut shells at the next door cat. The next door cat purred still more loudly . . . The visitor was going to have a quiet little talk with his father after tea tomorrow . . . By hook or by crook William decided to hear that quiet little talk. The only drawback to the plan was that the morning-room contained no possible place of concealment for eavesdroppers . . .

"William dear, this is Mr Cranthorpe-Cranborough, a relation of ours who has come to pay us a little visit," said Mrs Brown.

William looked up.

The first thing that struck you about Mr Cranthorpe-Cranborough was his bigness, and the second was his smile. Mr Cranthorpe-Cranborough's smile was as large and full as himself. His teeth were so over-crowded that when he smiled it almost seemed as if some were in danger of dropping out. He placed a large hand upon William's head.

"So *this* is the little man," he said.

"Uh – huh?" said William.

"Oh, his *manners*," groaned Ethel turning her eyes towards the sky.

"A-ha," said Mr Cranthorpe-Cranborough, smiling like a playful ogre, "you may safely leave his manners to *me*. I'm used to teaching little boys their manners."

William took a nut out of his pocket and cracked it.

"William!" groaned Mrs Brown.

William took out a handful of nuts and handed it to Mr Cranthorpe-Cranborough.

"Have one?" he said politely.

"Er – no, I thank you," said Mr Cranthorpe-Cranborough. Then he smiled the very full smile again, "But I'd like a talk with you, my little man."

His little man turned a sphinx-like countenance to him and cracked another nut.

"How far have you got in Arithmetic?" asked Mr Cranthorpe-Cranborough.

"Uh-huh?" said William.

Ethel groaned.

"Fractions?" suggested Mr Cranthorpe-Cranborough.

William's whole attention was given to the inside of the nut that he had just cracked.

"Bad!" he said indignantly, "an' I paid twopence for 'em . . . I'll take it back to the shop."

"Decimals?" said Mr Cranthorpe-Cranborough.

"No, Brazils," said William succinctly.

"I think perhaps it would be better if we left them," murmured Mrs Brown faintly, and she and Ethel departed, Ethel murmuring wildly, "His *manners!*"

"And what about History?" said Mr Cranthorpe-Cranborough.

William, investigating another nut, seemed to have no views on history.

Mr Cranthorpe-Cranborough cleared his throat, smiled his large fat smile and said, "Ha!" to attract William's attention. He failed, however. William's whole attention was given to throwing bits of his bad nut at the next door cat who had disappeared at the first intrusion of the grown-ups, but had now returned and was again purring loudly.

"What are the dates of Queen Elizabeth?" said Mr Cranthorpe-Cranborough.

"Uh?" said William absently, "here's another of 'em bad an' chargin' *twopence* for 'em! Haven't they gotta *nerve!*"

Mr Cranthorpe-Cranborough gave up the attempt.

"I'm going to have a nice little talk with your father after tea, my little man," he said.

William cracked a nut in (partial) silence and threw the shells at the cat. Then he said casually, "I s'pose they've told you he's deaf? He gets awful mad if people don't shout loud enough. You've gotta shout *awful* loud to make him hear."

"Er – your mother never mentioned it," said Mr Cranthorpe-Cranborough taken aback.

"No," said William mysteriously, "an' don't say anythin' about it to her or to any of them. They don' like folks mentionin' it. They're – they're – sort of sens'tive about it."

"Oh!" said Mr Cranthorpe-Cranborough still more taken aback. Then he recovered himself. "Now let's have a few dates," he said briskly.

"Yes, dates is more sense," said William with interest, "you can look at 'em before you buy 'em to see if they're bad. That's the worst of nuts. You can't see 'em through the shells."

Viciously he threw the defaulting nut at the cat who remembered suddenly a previous engagement on the other side of the fence and disappeared.

While Mr Cranthorpe-Cranborough was engaged in recovering himself for a fresh assault upon William's ignorance Ethel appeared.

"Will you come in to tea now?" she said to the visitor with a sweet smile.

Mr Cranthorpe-Cranborough responded to the best of his ability with his fullest smile.

William, interested by the phenomenon, went up to his bedroom to practise, but found that he had not enough teeth to get the full effect.

When he descended he found his father in the hall hanging up his coat and hat.

"You're back early, father, aren't you?" said William innocently.

"With your usual intelligence, my son," said William's father, "you have divined aright . . . Where's Mr What's-his-name?"

"Having tea in the drawing-room, father," said William.

Mr Brown went into the morning-room. William followed him.

"Have you – met him?" said Mr Brown.

"Yes," said William.

"Er – do you like him?"

"He's very deaf," said William.

"Deaf?"

"Yes . . . you've gotta shout ever so hard to make him hear."

"Good Heavens!" groaned Mr Brown.

"An' *he* shouts very hard, too, like what deaf people do, you know, with not hearin' themselves – but he dun't like you *sayin'* anythin' about him bein' deaf, but he likes you jus' shoutin'. They're havin' their tea now. He's given 'em quite sore throats already."

Mr Brown groaned again but at that minute entered Mrs Brown and the guest. She performed a rapid introduction and departed. William had already disappeared. He had gone round to the front lawn and was sitting there leaning against the house cracking nuts. Just above his head was the open window of the morning-room. It was not possible from that position to overhear a conversation carried on in normal voices in the morning-room, but William hoped that he had assured that this conversation would be carried on in abnormal voices. His hopes were justified. His father's voice raised to a bellow reached him.

"Won't you sit down?"

And Mr Cranthorpe-Cranborough's in a hoarse shout: "Thanks so much."

"Now about this school—" yelled his father.

"Exactly," bellowed Mr Cranthorpe-Cranborough. "I

hope to open it in the spring. I should like to include your son among the first numbers – special terms of course."

There was a pause, then William's father spoke in a voice of thunder.

"Very good of you."

"Not at all," bellowed Mr Cranthorpe-Cranborough.

"He's – perhaps I'd better prepare you . . ." boomed Mr Brown's voice making the very window panes rattle in their frames, "he – he doesn't quite conform to type. He's a bit – individualistic."

Mr Cranthorpe-Cranborough drew in his breath, then with a mighty effort bellowed:

"But he ought to conform to type. It's only a matter of training . . . I'm most anxious to include your son on our roll when we open next spring."

Purple in the face Mr Brown yelled:

"Very good of you."

William, whose conscience never allowed him to do any more eavesdropping than was absolutely necessary to his plans, arose and thoughtfully cracking his last nut, walked round the house. At the side door he came across his mother and Ethel clinging together in terror.

"What *has* happened," his mother was saying hysterically, "why are they shouting at each other like that? What *has* happened?"

"They must be quarrelling!" groaned Ethel. A re-echoing bellow from Mr Brown (who was really only saying, "Very good of you" again) made the house shake and Ethel screamed, "They'll be *fighting* in a minute . . . What *shall* we do?"

Mrs Brown noticed William and made an effort to control herself.

"Where are you going, William?"

William, his hands deep in his pockets, answered non-chalantly. "Down to the village to buy a stick of liquorice," he said.

He walked down to the village very thoughtfully.

So *that* was it . . . they were going to send him to that man's school, were they? Huh! . . . *were* they? William for one had made up his mind that they were not, but just for a minute he was not sure how he could prevent them. Silently he considered various plans. None seemed suitable. Open opposition was, he knew, useless. In open opposition he had no chance against his family. But there must surely be other ways . . .

Mrs Brown had once stayed in Eastbourne where she had watched a neat little crocodile of neat little boys walking in a straight and tidy line past her house every day and the sight had impressed her. The thought of William walking like that – a neat and tidy component of a neat and tidy line talking politely to his partner, keeping just behind the boy in front, with plastered hair and shiny shoes, walking sedately – was an alluring and startling picture when compared with the William of the present, leaping over fences, diving into ditches, shinning up trees, dragging his toes in the dust, shouting . . . Mrs Brown had a vague idea that some mysterious change of spirit came over a boy on entering the portals of a boarding-school transforming him from a young savage to a perfect little gentleman, and she would have liked to see this change take place in William. Moreover Mr Cranthorpe-Cranborough had distinctly mentioned "special fees".

Mr Brown had no very strong feelings on the subject. He was prepared to leave it all to his wife. The only two people concerned who had any very strong feelings about it were

Mr Cranthorpe-Cranborough and William. Mr Cranthorpe-Cranborough wanted to fill his new school. He did not consider William to be very promising material but he couldn't afford at the present juncture to be too particular about material . . . And William had very strong feeling on the subject indeed. William could not even contemplate life divorced from the beloved fields and woods of his native village, his beloved Outlaws and Jumble his mongrel.

On returning home William found his father in the hall.

"What the dickens do you mean," said his father irritably and hoarsely, "by telling me the fellow was deaf? He's no more deaf than I am."

William opened wide eyes of innocent surprise.

"Isn't he, father?" he said, "I'm awfully sorry."

William's father, upon whom William's looks of innocence and surprise were always completely wasted, moved his hand to his throat with an involuntary spasm of pain.

"No, he isn't," he said brokenly, "and you knew perfectly well he wasn't. Your over-exuberant sense of humour needs a little pruning, my boy, and if I hadn't got the worst sore throat I've had in years I'd prune it for you here and now."

William moved hastily out of the danger zone still murmuring apologies. He went to the morning-room where he found Mr Cranthorpe-Cranborough. Mr Cranthorpe-Cranborough addressed him, also brokenly.

"Your father doesn't seem to be very deaf, William," he whispered hoarsely, "I spoke to him in quite an ordinary tone of voice towards the end of our conversation and he seemed to hear all right."

William fixed unfaltering eyes upon him.

"Yes, then your voice must be the kind he hears nat'rul. He does hear some sorts nat'rul. He hears all ours nat'ral."

With this cryptic remark he withdrew leaving Mr Cranthorpe-Cranborough looking thoughtful.

The next morning Mr Cranthorpe-Cranborough asked William to go for a walk with him. "William and I," he said pleasantly to Mrs Brown, "must get to know each other."

William emerged from Mrs Brown's hands for the walk almost repellently clean and tidy. Mrs Brown was determined that William should make a good impression on Mr Cranthorpe-Cranborough.

For a time William walked in silence and Mr Cranthorpe-Cranborough talked. He talked about the glorious historical monuments of England and the joys of early rising and the fascination of decimals and H.C.F.'s and the beauty of all foreign languages. He warmed to William as he talked for William seemed to be drinking in his words almost avidly. William's solemn eyes never left his face. He could not know, of course, that William was not listening to a word he said but was engaged in trying to count his teeth . . .

"Now which of our grand national buildings have you seen?" said Mr Cranthorpe-Cranborough, returning to his first theme.

"Uh-huh?" said William who thought he'd got to thirty, but kept having to start again because they moved about so.

"I say, which of our grand national buildings have you seen?" said Mr Cranthorpe-Cranborough more distinctly.

"Oh," said William bringing his thoughts with an effort from Mr Cranthorpe-Cranborough's teeth to the less interesting one of our grand national buildings, "I've never been to races," said William sadly.

"Races?" said Mr Cranthorpe-Cranborough in surprise.

"Yes . . . you was talking about the Grand National, wasn't you?"

"Were, William, were," corrected Mr Cranborough.

"I'm not quite sure where," admitted William, "but I know a man what won some money on it last year."

"You misunderstand me, William," said Mr Cranborough rather irritably, "I'm referring to such places as Westminster Abbey and the Houses of Parliament."

"Oh," said William with waning interest, "I thought you was goin' to talk about racin'."

"Were, William, *were*."

"At the Grand National."

"No, William . . . no," he was finding conversation with William rather difficult, "have you never visited such places as Hampton Court?"

A gleam of interest came into William's face and he temporarily abandoned his self-imposed task of counting Mr Cranborough's teeth.

"Yes," he said, "I once went *there*. I remember 'cause there was a man there what told us it was haunted. Said a ghost of someone used to go downstairs there. Huh!"

William's final ejaculation was one of contemptuous amusement. But Mr Cranthorpe-Cranborough's face grew serious. His teeth receded from view almost entirely.

"No, no, William," he said reprovingly, "you must not make fun of such things. Indeed you must not. They are – they are not to be treated lightly. The fact that you have *seen* none is not proof that there *are* none . . . far from it . . . Believe me, William – though I have seen none myself I have friends who have."

"Didn't it scare 'em stiff?" said William with interest, and added dramatically, "rattlin' an' groanin' an' such-like."

Mr Cranborough was too much absorbed in his subject to correct William's phraseology.

"It does not – er – rattle or groan, William. It is the figure of a lady of the fifteenth century, and everyone does not see it. It is indeed a sinister omen to see it. Some evil always befalls those who see it. Sinister, William, means on the left hand, and used in the sense in which we use it, is a reference to the omens of the days of the Romans."

"Doesn't it *do* anythin' to 'em?" said William, disappointed by the lack of enterprise betrayed by the ghost, and left completely cold by the derivation of the word sinister.

"No," said Mr Cranborough, "it just *appears – but* the one who sees it, and only one person sees it on each occasion, invariably suffers some catastrophe. It is not wise, of course, to allow one's thoughts to *dwell* upon such things but it is not wise either to treat them entirely with contempt . . . Let us now turn our thoughts to brighter things . . . Do you keep a collection of – the flora of the neighbourhood, William?"

"No," admitted William, "I've never caught any of *them*. Didn't know there was any about. But I've got some caterpillars."

When William approached the morning-room just before lunch there were there his mother and Ethel and Robert, his grown-up brother. As William entered he heard his mother whisper:

"I think the time has come to tell him."

William entered, negligently toying with a handful of marbles.

"William," said his mother, "we have something to tell you."

"Uh-huh?" said William still apparently absorbed by his marbles.

"Oh, his *manners!*" groaned Ethel.

"This cousin of your father's," said his mother, "is really the headmaster of a boys' boarding-school and we *think* . . .

though nothing's yet arranged . . . that we're going to send *you* to his school next spring. *Won't* it be nice?"

They all looked at William with interest to see how he should receive this startling news.

William received it as though it had been some casual comment on the weather.

"Uh-huh," he said absently, as he continued to toy negligently with his marbles.

He had the satisfaction of seeing his family thoroughly taken aback by his reception of the news.

He was very silent during lunch. He had not yet formed any definite plan of action beyond the negative plan of pretending to acquiesce. He could see that his attitude mystified them and the knowledge was a great consolation to him.

After lunch Mr Cranthorpe-Cranborough, who by now looked upon the addition of William's name to his roll of members as a certainty, went into the garden and Mrs Brown went to lie down. William, after strolling aimlessly about the house, joined Ethel in the drawing-room. She was, however, not alone in the drawing-room. Moyna Greene in an elaborate fourteenth century dress of purple and silver was with her.

"You look perfectly sweet, Moyna," Ethel was saying, "but I think the ruffle *does* want altering just here."

"I thought it did," said Moyna, "I'll do it now if I may. May I borrow your work basket? Thanks." She slipped off her ruffle.

"Let me help," said Ethel.

Just then the housemaid entered.

"Mrs Bott called to see you, Miss," she said to Ethel.

Ethel groaned and turned to Moyna.

"Oh, my dear . . . I'll be as quick as I can, but you know what she is . . . She'll keep me ages. You *won't* run away, will you?"

"No," promised the purple and silver vision.

"I'll tell you what you might do," said Ethel. 'Go and let old Jenkins see you. I think he's in the greenhouse. I told him you were going as a fourteenth century lady and he said, 'Eh, her'll look rare prutty. I wish I could see her' – so he'd be so bucked if you would."

"All right," said Moyna, "I'll just finish this ruffle and then I'll go out to him."

"And I'll be as quick as I can," said Ethel, "but you know what she is."

William went quietly out of doors. His face was bright with inspiration and stern with resolve. First of all he satisfied himself that old Jenkins really was in the greenhouse.

Jenkins turned upon him as soon as he saw him in the doorway. Between old Jenkins and young William no love was lost.

"You touch one of my grapes, Master William," he said threateningly, "an' I'll tell your pa the minute he comes home to-night, I will. I grow these grapes for your ma an' pa – not you."

"I don' want any of your grapes, Jenkins," said William with a short laugh expressive of amused surprise at the idea. "Good gracious, what should *I* want with your ole grapes?"

Whereupon he departed with a swagger leaving old Jenkins muttering furiously, and went to join Mr Cranthorpe-Cranborough who was comfortably ensconced in a deck chair at the further end of the lawn wooing sleep. He had almost wooed it when William appeared and sat down noisily at his feet, and said in a tone that put any further wooing of sleep entirely out of the question:

"Hello, Mr Cranborough."

Mr Cranborough greeted William shortly and without enthusiasm. He did not want William. He did not like William. His interest in William began and ended with the special fees which he hoped William's parents might be induced to pay him – "special" in quite a different sense from the one in which Mrs Brown understood it. He had been quite happy without William and he meant his manner to convey this fact to William. But William was not sensitive to fine shades of manner.

"I've been thinkin'," he said slowly, "'bout what you said this mornin'.."

"Ah," said Mr Cranthorpe-Cranborough, touched despite himself and thinking what a gift for dealing with the young he must possess to have made an impression upon such unpromising material as this boy's mind, and how one should never despair of material however unpromising.

"About what, my boy?" he said with interest, "the History? the French? the Arithmetic?"

"No," said William simply, "the ghost."

"Oh," said Mr Cranthorpe-Cranborough, "but – er – you should not allow your mind to *run* on such subjects, my boy."

"No," said William, "it's not runnin' on 'em. But I've just remembered somethin' about this house."

"What?" said Mr Cranthorpe-Cranborough.

William carefully selected a juicy blade of grass and began to chew it.

"Oh, it's prob'ly nothin'," he said carelessly, "but what you said this mornin' made me think of it, that's all."

William was adept at whetting people's curiosity.

"But what *was* it?" said Mr Cranthorpe-Cranborough irritably, "what *was* it?"

"Well, p'raps I'd better not mention it," said William, "you said we oughtn't to let it run on our minds."

"I insist on your telling me," said Mr Cranthorpe-Cranborough.

"Oh, it's nothin' much," said William again, "only a sort of *story* about this house."

"*What* sort of a story?" insisted Mr Cranthorpe-Cranborough.

MR CRANTHORPE-CRANBOROUGH GAZED, ACROSS THE LAWN
AND HIS JAW DROPPED. "LOOK!" HE GASPED TO
WILLIAM. "WHO'S THAT?"

"Well," said William as though reluctantly, "some folks say that an ole house use to be here jus' where this house is now an' that a lady of the fourteenth century was killed in it once an' some folks say they've seen her. I don' b'lieve it," he ended carelessly, "*I've* never seen her."

Mr Cranthorpe-Cranborough's interest was aroused.

"What is this – this lady supposed to look like, my boy?" he said.

"She's dressed in purple and silver," said William, "with a long train an' a ruffle thing round her neck an' very black hair, and she's s'posed to walk out of that window over there," and he pointed to the drawing-room window, "and then go across the lawn behind those trees," he pointed to the trees which hid the greenhouse from view.

"And you say that people profess to have *seen* her?" said Mr Cranthorpe-Cranborough.

"Oh, yes," said William.

THE FIGURE OF MISS GREEN CROSSED THE LAWN AND
DISAPPEARED BEHIND THE TREES.

"And what does her coming portend?"

"Uh?" said William.

"What – what *happens* to those who see her?" repeated Mr Cranthorpe-Cranborough impatiently.

At that moment Miss Moyna Greene, having finished and donned the ruffle, stepped out of the drawing-room window on to the lawn in all her glory of purple and silver. Mr Cranthorpe-Cranborough gazed at her and his jaws dropped open.

"Look!" he gasped to William, "who's that?"

"Who's what?" said William gazing around innocently.

Miss Moyna Greene passed slowly to the middle of the lawn. Mr Cranthorpe-Cranborough's eyes, bulging with amazement, followed her. So did his trembling forefinger.

"There . . ." he hissed, "just there."

William stared straight at Miss Moyna Greene.

"I don't see anyone," he said.

Drops of perspiration stood out on Mr Cranthorpe-Cranborough's brow. He took out a large silk handkerchief and mopped it. The figure of Miss Moyna Greene crossed the lawn and disappeared behind the trees . . .

Mr Cranthorpe-Cranborough gave a gasp.

"Er – what did you say the – er – the sight of the vision is supposed to portend, William?" he said faintly. "What – what *happens* to those who see it?"

"Oh, I don' suppose anyone's really seen it," said William carelessly. "I never have. I think they've simply made it up – purple dress an' ruffle an' all – but it's *s'posed* to mean very bad luck for the one who sees it."

"W – w – what kind of bad luck?" stammered Mr Cranthorpe-Cranborough, whose ruddy countenance had faded to a dull grey.

"Well," said William confidentially, "it's s'posed to be seen by one of two people together an' the one what *sees* it is s'posed to be goin' to have some *very* bad luck *through* the other – the one what was with him when he saw it, but what didn't see it. The bad luck's s'posed always to come *through* the one what doesn't see it but what's *with* the one what *does*."

Through the trees William spied the figure of Miss Moyna Greene who had evidently left Jenkins and was returning to the drawing-room.

"An' folks *say*," added William carelessly, "that it's worst of *all* if you see it twice – once going from the house and once comin' to it."

The figure of Miss Moyna Greene emerged from the trees and passed slowly on to the lawn. Mr Cranthorpe-Cranborough watched it in stricken silence. Then he said to William with an unconvincing attempt at nonchalance:

"You – you don't see anyone on the lawn, William, do you?" he said.

Again William looked straight at Miss Moyna Greene.

"No," he said innocently. "There ain't no one there."

Miss Moyna Greene disappeared through the drawing-room window.

"All the bad luck," repeated William artlessly, "s'posed to come *from* the one they're with when they see it, but I don't b'lieve anyone ever *has* seen it if you ask me."

He looked up at Mr Cranthorpe-Cranborough. Mr Cranthorpe-Cranborough was still yellow and still perspiring. He took out his handkerchief and mopped his brow.

"You don' look very well," said William kindly, "can I do anythin' for you?"

Mr Cranthorpe-Cranborough brought his eyes with an effort from the direction in which Miss Moyna Greene had

vanished to William. And his expression changed. He
seemed to realise for the first time the full import of his
vision.

"Yes, William," he said with fear and shrinking in his
manner. "You can – er – you can fetch me a railway time-
table, my dear boy, if you'll be so good."

William and Ethel and Robert had gone to bed.

Mr and Mrs Brown sat in the drawing-room alone.

"He went very suddenly, didn't he?" said Mr Brown, "I
thought I'd find him here to-night."

"I can't understand it," said Mrs Brown, "he behaved
most *strangely*. *Suddenly* came in and said he was going.
Gave no reason and was most *peculiar* in his manner."

"And you didn't arrange anything about William going
there?"

"I tried to. I said should we consider it settled, but he said
he was afraid he'd have no room for William, after all. I
suggested putting him on a waiting list, but he said he'd no
room on his waiting list either. He wouldn't even stay to
discuss it. He went off to the station at once though I told
him he'd have to wait half an hour for a train. And the last
thing he said was that he was sorry but he'd *no* room for
William. He said it several times. So strange after his offering
to take him at a special price."

"Very strange," said Mr Brown slowly. "He was – all right
at lunch you say?"

"Quite. He was talking then as if William were going."

"And what did he do after lunch?"

"He went into the garden to rest."

"And who was with him?"

"No one . . . Oh, except William for a few minutes."

"Ah," said Mr Brown, and remembered the sphinx-like

look upon William's face when he said Good-night to him. "I'd give a good deal to have been present at those few minutes – but the secret, whatever it was, will die with William, I suppose. William possesses the supreme gift of being able to keep his own counsel."

"Are you sorry, dear, that William's not going to a boarding-school?"

"I don't think I am," said Mr Brown.

"I should have thought you'd have found it so nice and quiet without him."

"Doubtless I should. But it would also have been extremely dull."

Just William's World
A Pictorial Map

Kenneth Waller

Illustrated by Gillian Clements

The first-ever map of William's village, with every
important feature shown in full-colour pictorial
form.

£3.99

M

The William Companion

Mary Cadogan

with David Schutte

The William stories occupy thirty-eight books; this
Companion provides an A–Z of who's who and
what's what in the saga, placing many apparently
disparate incidents in context, and providing
atmospheric and amusing studies of hundreds of
characters.

£14.95

M

School is a Waste of Time and other ritings by Just William

Kenneth Waller

Illustrated by Thomas Henry

Originally published in magazines in the '20s and
'30s, this collection gathers together in book form
William's own views on such important issues as
education, careers, and of course, civilizashun.

£3.50

M

The Just William Diary 1995

Richmal Crompton

Illustrated by Thomas Henry

The diary for William enthusiasts, with numerous
quotations from the irrepressible eleven-year-old,
and extracts from the stories – all liberally
illustrated with Thomas Henry's drawings.

£3.99 (inc VAT)

M